The Samaritan Bueno

by

Jack Weyland

Published and Distributed by:

Granite Publishing and Distributions, LLC
868 North 1430 West
Orem, UT 84057
(801) 229-9023 Toll Free (800) 574-5779
www.granitebooks.com

Cover Design by Tania Finn
Page Layout and Design by Myrna M. Varga

ISBN: 978-1-59936-042-3
Library of Congress Control Number: 2009929524

First Printing: June 2009

1 3 5 7 9 10 8 6 4 2

Printed in the United States of America

The Samaritan Bueno

Chapter One

They say everyone has talents. Maybe that would have also applied to Chad, Jonathan, and me. Our main talent was fouling up our ward youth leaders' plans. It had been that way since Chad moved into the ward four years earlier. The three of us lived within a half a block of each other in the small rural town of Milford, Utah.

Like when we were fourteen and the youth decided to paint a widow's house. The three of us were told to mix the paint. When we asked our adviser if he wanted us to mix all the paint, he said yes—the red for the shutters, the blue for the house, and the brown for the rafters. We dumped all of the paint into a large garbage can and mixed it. The resulting color was the shade of gray that reminds you of death. Our adviser was speechless for a long time, although his face turned a bright red and the veins in his neck were sticking out. Finally he gained enough composure to say, "Thank you very much! If you really want to help us some more, go home and don't come back!" As a parting gift, he even gave us the garbage can and the paint.

When we were fifteen, one of our quorum projects was to weed a widow's garden. But it's not that easy to tell a plant from a weed. At least for us it wasn't. The good news is that, when we finished, her garden had no weeds. The bad news is it had no flowers either.

But now we were seniors in high school and we hadn't messed up anything for at least a year. Near Christmas, our bishop proposed another program. "Let's bring the youth of the ward together, have them fill boxes with food and a few presents, and then send them out to deliver the boxes to the needy families in our ward. This will help our youth experience the true meaning of Christmas."

And so, at eight-thirty on a Wednesday night, a few days before Christmas, Jonathan Miller, Chad Anderson, and me, Daniel Winchester, were given a Christmas box to deliver. Our priest quorum adviser offered to drive us, but Chad said we'd get done quicker if we didn't have to ride around with others who also needed to deliver boxes. The address we were given was near where we lived. It was a neighborhood that was a mix of a few historic mansions, mingled with dumpy, three- and four-family rental houses. And some regular homes too, like where we lived.

It had snowed a few days earlier but then warmed up, so the only snow left was where the plows had piled it up on the sides of the streets.

"I'm getting bored with Christmas," Chad said as we started to walk the three blocks to the address we'd been given. Chad was the biggest so he was carrying the box. "It's the same thing every year. I mean, every Christmas Eve my dad reads the Christmas story to us. I've heard it so many times. It's always the same, year after year. I complained about it once and my mom goes, 'But Chad, the Christmas story changes from year to year.' Yeah, right, like some years he's born in a Super Eight Motel, and other years instead of shepherds coming to see him it's like a group of Boy Scouts from Alabama. Just once I'd like the innkeeper to say, 'Hey, no problem, we've got plenty of room.' "

"What'd your mom mean about the Christmas story changing from year to year?" Jonathan asked. Of the three of us, he was the sincere one. Like the time we were trying to decide if we should toilet-paper our bishop's big tree in front of his house, and Jonathan said, "This will only make more work for the bishop. Is this what we really want to do? Wouldn't it be better to mow his lawn?" Chad and I always hated it when Jonathan's goodness surfaced.

A few minutes later we were standing in front of a small house.

"Are you sure this is the right place?" Jonathan asked.

"Yeah, sure, where else could it be?" I said. "Let's just drop it off and then get out of here."

We approached the house, and I knocked on the door.

A tired-looking woman answered our knock. Her skin was dark brown, and she had long, straight black hair. Two cute little kids clung to her skirt and peered out around her legs at us.

"Hi, there," I said. "We're from the Church. This is for you," I said, handing her the box. "Merry Christmas."

Her face lit up as she saw what was in the box, and she let out a stream of words in Spanish.

As we left her house, we all felt good. "That's wasn't so bad, was it?" I said.

"Yeah, it was okay," Chad said.

"Hey, Jonathan, what did she say?" I asked.

"How should I know?"

"She was speaking Spanish, wasn't she? Your mom's from Mexico, right?"

"Guatemala."

"Same thing. So you should be able to understand what she said."

"Where did your ancestors come from?" Jonathan asked me.

"Scotland and Sweden."

"Do you speak Swedish?"

"No, of course not, but it's not the same thing," I said.

"Why isn't it the same thing?"

"My family came here like a hundred years ago. Not like your mom. When did she come here?"

"When she was six years old."

"So you should be able to speak Spanish."

"I know a little, but not very much."

"I know Spanish," Chad said. "Taco, tortilla, enchilada, salsa."

"Hey, look," Jonathan said, pointing to the house next door to the one where we'd dropped off the Christmas box.

We could see inside the house because there were no drapes or blinds over the windows. A woman was washing the windows from the inside with her three kids helping her.

"That woman was at church last week," Jonathan said. "I can't remember her name, but she talked to my dad about getting their membership records transferred. They look like they could use a Christmas box too. I wonder why we didn't deliver it there. . ." He stopped talking. "Hey, wait a minute, let me see the paper with the name and address on it."

I was about to hand the list to Jonathan when Chad grabbed it. He read the address and then bopped my head with his hand. "Way to go, Einstein," he said. "We gave the box to the wrong address. It was supposed to go to 2440, not 2436."

They both glared at me.

"Hey, anybody can make a mistake," I said. "We'll just go back and get it."

"How long is this going to take?" Chad complained. "I didn't want to do this tonight anyway. I'm going home. I've got a lot to do tonight."

"Like what?" I asked.

"My brother's home from college. We rented a bunch of movies to watch, and we've only got three days before we have to take them back."

"I need to go home too," Jonathan said. "I haven't practiced yet." He played the violin.

"Look, you guys, you're not going anywhere until we're done here," I said. "Besides, it's not going to take that long. The woman must know this was a mistake, so all we need to do is knock on her door, ask for the box, and then drop it off where it was supposed to go."

We approached the first house again. I knocked on the door, and the same woman came to the door. I felt stupid. "Hi, it's us again. You know what? We made a, well, a little mistake, I guess you could say," I stammered. "The box we gave you is actually supposed to go next door," I said, pointing over my shoulder.

The woman smiled and invited us in. Or at least I think that's what she said. She moved some things out of the doorway so we could get in.

She was wearing a thin dress that was kind of tattered and old-looking and had a ratty old sweater around her shoulders. In the living room, in front of a small black and white TV, the two small children were huddled together with a blanket around them, eating green beans out of one of the cans we'd just delivered. It was cold in the house.

"Hey, weren't they supposed to wait until Christmas?" Chad asked.

"What do we do now?" Jonathan asked. "She's looking at us like she expects us to say something."

"Let's sing *Silent Night*," I said.

"Are you crazy? I'm not singing," Chad complained.

"Why do you always have to be dragging your feet?" I shot back. "Just once can't you help us here?"

We sang *Silent Night*. By the time we finished, the woman had tears in her eyes. "We've got to find a way to tell her she's not supposed to have the box," I said.

"My brother took Spanish in high school," Jonathan said. "I know where his Spanish-English dictionary is. That might help us."

"Let's go get it then," I said.

Before we left, I wanted to make sure she didn't use any of the other food in the box. Using my hands to emphasize what I was saying, I said very slowly, "Look, whatever you do, don't cook the turkey, okay?"

She shrugged her shoulders.

"Gobble like a turkey, Chad," I said.

"Why would I do that?"

"So she doesn't cook the turkey. Gobble like a turkey. You're good at things like that."

Chad got down on his knees and flapped his arms and gobbled.

The children started laughing hard. They apparently thought Chad was hilarious.

Jonathan looked at his watch. He had like an eating disorder, except it wasn't about food. It was about practicing his stupid violin.

The woman's two kids got off the couch and onto the floor next to Chad and began gobbling too.

"No cook turkey, no cook turkey," I said, speaking slowly and loudly.

The woman repeated, "No cook turkey."

"She's got it!" Chad said. "Let's go now."

"Yeah, except she has no clue what it means," Jonathan added. "We'd better go get the dictionary."

"We're going to get a dictionary, okay?" I shouted at the woman. "And then we'll be back."

"*Dictionario?*" she asked.

"Si," Chad said. "*Dictionario.*"

Outside, he said to us. "Spanish isn't that hard. Is it? You just add an *o* to every word."

A minute later we were hurrying on our way to Jonathan's house. "I can't believe her kids are eating cold green beans without anything else," I said. "I hate green beans."

"People from Mexico love green beans," Chad said enthusiastically. The less Chad knew about a subject, the more enthusiastic he was about it.

"What are you talking about?" I challenged.

"No, it's true. Every year they have like a green bean festival. I think it was on the Discovery Channel once."

"Since when did you ever watch the Discovery Channel?" Jonathan asked. He was someone who actually *did* watch that channel. And took notes.

"Hey, I do a lot of things people don't know about," Chad said. "Like one time I went to a choir concert with my mom and dad."

"Did you like it?" Jonathan asked.

"Not really, but my mom bribed me with candy, so it wasn't too bad. When the candy was gone, we left."

"That woman was so happy about the box we gave her," Jonathan said.

"Yeah, but she must have known it wasn't meant for her," I said. "I mean, why would we give her a box of food for Christmas? We don't know her, and she's probably not even a member of the church."

"I think maybe other churches do that kind of thing. You know, randomly give Christmas boxes to anybody," Chad said.

"Maybe so," I said.

A minute later I asked what for me was a sensitive question. "Jonathan, does Michelle ever talk about me?" I asked.

Michelle, a sophomore, was Jonathan's younger sister.

"No, why should she? And why would you care if she did?"

"I don't care. I was just curious, that's all."

Maybe because she took dancing lessons, Michelle had a graceful way of walking. Her eyes were dark brown. Her hair was also brown and very long. And she played the piano. Of course you'd expect musical ability from any kid in Jonathan's family. Their mom used to play violin in the Utah Symphony before she got married.

Michelle and I had never talked much. Whenever Chad, Jonathan, and I entered the house, she would always escape to her room. I don't blame her. When Chad talked, the dishes rattled.

"You're talking about Johnny B's sister?" Chad asked. He couldn't bring himself to use such a formal name as Jonathan. Since Jonathan's middle name was Braxton, Chad called him Johnny B.

"Yeah, so what if I am? Is that like a crime?" I shot back.

"You like her?" Chad teased.

"I didn't say I liked her, did I? I was just wondering if she ever said anything about me."

"What would she say?" Chad asked.

"Nothing! Look, just forget it, okay?"

Imitating a little girl's voice, Chad chanted, "I just love Cowboy Dan and his blond hair, especially his baby blue eyes."

The reason Chad called me Cowboy Dan is because my last name is Winchester. One time when I was over at Chad's house, his dad told us about the Winchester rifle. He told us that historians called it the rifle that won the West. Ever since then Chad had been calling me Cowboy Dan or just Cowboy.

"Knock it off, Chad! I mean it."

Jonathan's family wasn't home, and the three of us went directly to Jonathan's brother's room and found the Spanish-English dictionary.

"What are we going to say?" Chad asked.

"I don't know. We'd better write it out first," I said.

"How about this? 'We want our food back pronto!'" Chad said.

"No, that sounds like a threat," Jonathan said. "We need to tell her why we want it back. How about this? 'Excuse us, but we were out delivering boxes of food to needy members of our church. We made a mistake giving you the food. We should have given it to the house next door. So now we'd like it back. You don't have to give back the green beans. That can be our special Christmas gift to you, but we do want everything else back right away because it's late and some of us need to go home and practice.' "

I glared at him. "What you just said would take us three weeks to translate. I haven't even found the word for turkey yet."

"It's turkio," Chad said confidently.

"Yeah, right," I grumbled.

"Let's just get this over with," Chad complained. "I'm missing my first movie."

"Quit complaining!" I shot back. "The bishop sent us out to do a job, and we're not quitting until we've done it. Let's just say something easy, like 'Not your food. Give it back.'"

"I think *comida* is the Spanish word for food," Jonathan said.

"What's the Spanish word for no?" Chad asked.

"No," Jonathan said.

Chad smiled. "You see there? Spanish is easy."

"How do I say 'not your food'?" I asked.

"I have no idea," Jonathan said. "We could say, 'We need the food.'"

"What's the word for need?" I asked.

"I don't know," Jonathan said. "But, you know what? I do know the word for want. It's *quiero*. So maybe we could say '*Quiero comida, por favor.*'"

"What does that mean?"Chad asked.

"I want food, please."

"Great, so then she'll cook us dinner," Chad said. "How do you say, 'Give us back the food we just gave you'?"

"Beats me," Jonathan said.

"Look, we're wasting time," Chad said. "Let's decide what we're going to say on the way over."

We headed back to the woman's house.

"Why don't we just let her have it all?" Chad asked. "It's just a few cans of green beans, some potatoes, some bread, some turkey, and a few presents."

"I agree with Chad," Jonathan said.

I couldn't face having to admit to the bishop we'd messed up again. "She's taking advantage of us, you know that, don't you?" I said.

"How do you figure?" Jonathan argued. "She opens the door, we give her a box of food, and she takes it. You think she was just lying in wait for someone to come by and give her a box of food by mistake?"

"Yeah, yeah, that's the way it was!" Chad said. "I saw a thing about it on TV. It's like this big crime ring! And every year they get away with as many as one hundred cans of green beans! Do you guys have any idea what the street value of that would be in L.A.?"

Jonathan burst out laughing.

I was mad at them both. "Look, every time we're asked to do something in the ward, we mess it up. The Laurels have lost all respect for us. So we're not messing this up too."

That silenced them for maybe thirty seconds. And then, under his breath, Chad said to Jonathan, "I wonder if the Three Wise Men ever had problems like this. Like if they gave it to the wrong stable. I can see it now. 'Hey, we want our myrrh back!'"

They laughed while I fumed.

"What exactly is a myrrh anyway?" Jonathan asked.

"Hey, you're the one who spends all his free time on Google," Chad said. "I bet you could look that up and give us a report."

"You guys shut up and let me think!" I grumbled.

"And now, for the first time in his life, Cowboy Dan is going to think!" Chad announced to anyone within a two block radius.

"How about this? 'The food's not for you. We want it back right now,'" I suggested.

"Forget what I said about Cowboy Dan here thinking," Chad teased.

"Chad, if you put half as much energy into actually trying to help instead of complaining all the time, we'd be done by now."

"What about the green beans?" Jonathan asked.

"She can have them, but she has to give everything else back," I said.

"What will we do if she won't give any of it back?" Jonathan asked.

"I know, I know!" Chad said. "We'll make her listen to your report on the history of the myrrh. She'll beg for mercy and give back the box."

We stopped under a street light and with the help of the dictionary worked out a message in Spanish. "*Comida no para usted. Quiero comida pronto,*" which we hoped said, "The food isn't for you. I want the food back right now!"

A few minutes later we stood on the sidewalk in front of her house, trying to work up the courage to go back into the house.

"Let's go," I said.

Chad shook his head. "You guys go ahead. I say let her have the stupid box. She and her kids need it bad."

"I agree with Chad," Jonathan said.

"All right, fine! I'll do it myself!" I snapped. "I don't need you guys anyway."

"We'll wait," Chad said.

I went up onto the porch and knocked on the door. The woman greeted me with a big smile and invited me in, as though I were a member of her family. As I stepped inside, I could smell turkey cooking. I looked into the kitchen. She'd cut off some of it and was frying it in a pan.

I looked down at the message in Spanish and cleared my throat.

A few minutes later I returned to Chad and Jonathan.

"Where's the box of food?" Chad asked.

"Actually, she was cooking the turkey when I got there."

"So, she can have it all, right?" Chad asked.

"Yeah, I guess so. I'll call the bishop when I get home and tell him what happened."

We started back to our neighborhood.

"Hey, wait a minute, weren't you wearing a coat when you went inside?" Chad asked.

"I must have left it there by mistake."

"You were wearing a BYU hoodie too," Chad added.

"I'll go back tomorrow and get it."

"Why not get it now?" Chad asked.

"I said I'd get it tomorrow, okay?" I grumbled.

We walked in silence.

"You gave away your coat and your hoodie?" Jonathan said.

"Look, I don't want to talk about it, okay?"

"Tell us why you did it, Cowboy," Chad asked.

"I thought the two kids could use 'em for pajamas. It's kind of cold in the house."

Nobody said anything for a while, and then I said, "When I went in, the kids were eating bread, with nothing on it."

"My mom makes this terrific strawberry jam," Jonathan said. "I'm sure I could sneak a jar out without her knowing about it."

"They'd need milk, too, and butter," I said.

"And a ball," Chad said. "Kids always need a ball to play with."

"How much money do you guys have? We'll need some for butter and milk."

"I've got a bunch of quarters in my room," Chad said.

"I have a few dollars in my dresser," Jonathan said.

"You're the only guy in America who says the word *dresser*," Chad teased.

"That's what it is."

"Do you dress in it?" Chad asked.

"No."

"Then it's not a dresser."

"What is it then?"

"It's a bunch of drawers stacked on top of each other."

When I walked in our house, my mom and dad were watching TV. I pretended to be hanging up my coat in the closet and then walked into the living room. My mom asked how things had gone delivering food to the needy. "Good," I said.

I went upstairs, looked through my things, found another sweat-shirt, put it on, reached in the back of my closet for an old coat, grabbed all the money I could find on my . . . well . . . dresser, and went back downstairs. I set the old coat by the door so my folks wouldn't ask where my new coat was.

"Chad needs help on his homework, so I'm going over to his house. I won't be long. Maybe half an hour."

"If you're going to be longer than that, give us a call," my mom said.

Now, years later, I ask myself why I didn't just tell my mom and dad what had happened. The reason is they would have assumed I wanted them to tell me what to do. But I didn't want advice. I knew what I wanted to do, and I didn't want them muddying the waters.

If I would have told my mom that I'd given away my coat and my favorite hoodie to what was probably an illegal alien family, she would have reminded me how much they'd cost, and my dad would have lectured me about that, if they were illegal aliens, my helping was a crime and I could be arrested. And if they found out that Chad and Jonathan and I were going to give them a few more things for Christmas, they would have told me there were agencies that took care of things like that.

All my life I'd been told that there were agencies in charge of things. So what agency gives kids jam and bread and milk and a ball so they can have a decent Christmas?

Chapter Two

can't remember much about Christmas that year. My mom and dad must have given me presents but I can't remember what they were. I'm sure they were very nice though and just what I wanted.

It was like what Chad had said. After a while Christmas is the same every year.

The day after Christmas my mom told me to clean my room. It was like "Okay, Christmas is over, Slave, now get to work."

At first I was grumpy about having to work, but once I started to go through my closet, I found games and toys I didn't use anymore but hadn't gotten around to throwing away. Like four jigsaw puzzles for kids and a Chutes and Ladders game and ten Matchbox cars—things I was sure our two Mexican kids would love. That's how I thought of them because I didn't know their names.

I started to wonder if that might also be true of Chad and Jonathan, so I called them. We agreed we'd pack up some things and take them to "our" kids.

I worried a little about getting it all out of the house without my mom asking what I was doing. But while she was on the phone with one of my older brothers, I filled a trash bag with all the things I was going to give away and carried it out to our trash can. When Chad showed up, he put it on his sled along with the presents he'd picked out.

Jonathan snuck his gifts out under his coat. When Chad saw him, he asked, "So, Johnny B, are you pregnant?"

Jonathan didn't even smile. "No."

Chad shook his head. "You been practicing violin again, right?"

"So?"

"You get totally zoned out when you practice the violin. It's worse than drugs."

"That's not true."

"It is. Trust me."

"Did you bring the dictionary?" I asked Jonathan.

"Yeah."

"Good."

"I told Michelle what we did," Jonathan said, glancing at me, "and how you gave away your coat and sweatshirt."

"Did she say anything?" I asked.

"No, but she got all teary eyed."

"She was probably just sorry for the two kids for getting such a ratty hoodie," Chad said.

"I don't think so. She goes, 'Dan is a good guy, isn't he?'"

Chad shook his head. "I definitely need to talk to that girl and set her straight. I'll tell her what you're really like."

"What am I really like?"

"You're a momma's boy. That pretty much says it all."

"What exactly does that mean?" Jonathan asked.

"It means Cowboy here is completely under the thumb of his mom. That's okay when you're eight, but now it's time to be a man with ideas of your own and not just an overgrown eight-year-old. Tell me, Cowboy, does your mom still tuck you in bed at night? I bet she does."

"You're so full of it," I said.

"You know I'm right."

We knocked on the door, expecting the mom and her kids to greet us with smiles and a big welcome, but I could tell she'd been crying. She let us in.

Jonathan and Chad carried our gifts into the living room and showed them to the kids. They were so happy and excited. Chad played Santa Claus, handing out the presents to them one at a time.

Their mom sat down at the kitchen table. She said some things that I couldn't understand, but from the way she said it, I was sure she was thanking us for bringing more gifts for her kids.

I borrowed Jonathan's dictionary and sat down with her at the table.

I realized I couldn't keep thinking of her as *Mexican Woman*, so I looked in a section that included useful phrases. "*Hola. Como te llamas?*"

My pronunciation was as good as I could do, knowing nothing about Spanish. I pronounced the greeting as "whole-ah." And of course everyone knows a llama is a South American animal, so I pronounced it that way.

She looked at me with an amused expression.

And then I noticed that in the book, below the text, it showed how to pronounce words. Apparently Mexicans have no use for the letter H, and a double LL sounds like a Y. When I repeated it the way the book said, she smiled through her tears and replied, "Maria Sanchez."

I decided I would tell her what our names were. I looked at the book, found the expression, and also the way it was supposed to sound. I pointed to myself and said, "*May yamo* Dan." That's the way it would sound in English, but, actually, it's written, "*Me llamo* Dan."

She nodded and tried to say my name the way I'd said it.

I called Chad over. "Listen very carefully. I want you to say '*May yamo* Chad.'"

"*May yamo Chad*," he said.

"*May yamo Maria Sanchez*."

"Her name is Maria Sanchez," I said.

Chad scoffed. "Right, like I wouldn't have been able to pick that up without your expert help."

The boy and girl came over. They were excited that we were talking Spanish.

"*Me llamo Kristina*," the girl said proudly.

"*Me llamo Gabriel*," the boy said.

"*Ola, Kristina! Ola, Gabriel*," I said. Spanish people spell it *Hola* though.

The kids then hit us with a flood of Spanish. Their mom said something to them, and then they quit and just said "*Hola*."

Chad and Jonathan went back to their game with the kids. Chad played every game like it was the game of the century, except now I knew he was doing his best to lose, even to stacking the deck so the kids would be sure to win.

It took me a while to come up with the Spanish version of "What's wrong?"

"*Problema?*" I asked. I was glad Chad wasn't listening in so he'd tell me again that Spanish was easy because all you had to do was add a vowel to the end of a word.

I handed her the dictionary, and she worked on giving me an answer.

"No money." She lifted her hands palm up, like "What am I supposed to do?"

I wondered if she didn't have money for rent. I looked up the word for house. "*Casa?*" I asked.

"*Si, casa.*"

Another look-up in the dictionary, and then I asked, "*No dinero para casa?*"

"*Si.*"

"Oh."

I wanted to know how much her rent was so I asked, "*Mucho dinero?*"

"*Si.*" She grabbed a piece of paper and wrote down 400.

"Four hundred dollars?"

"*Si.*"

There was a calendar on the wall. I pointed to it, and she pointed to the day her rent was due, which was in three days.

For the first time in my life I didn't know what to do. For most problems I couldn't solve, I went to my mom, or even sometimes to my dad, but I didn't see how I could do that with this. My dad was always complaining about all the Mexicans coming across the border, taking advantage of our schools and hospitals, so how could I talk to him? My dad's answer to illegal immigration was "Send them all back."

Maria Sanchez wasn't a member of the church so I was pretty sure the bishop wouldn't want to give her any fast offering funds to pay her rent.

This was too much of a problem for someone my age. I couldn't see how I could do anything for her so I didn't want to talk to her anymore because it was hard for me to admit there was something I couldn't make better. I mean, that's what guys do, right? Or at least what my dad did.

So I had to get away from it all so I could think. I sat down on an old couch and watched Chad and Jonathan play *Sorry* with Gabriel and Kristina.

The game ended with Chad pretending to be crushed to have lost the game. Which of course delighted Gabriel and Kristina.

"Double or nothing this game, okay?" Chad said. "You were just lucky the first game, but this time I'll totally smoke you." He stood up and did his evil genius imitation. "With this win I will rule the world!"

Gabriel might not have understood the words but he definitely understood he'd been given a challenge, and he loved it.

Kristina was tired of the game. She came over and crawled on my lap, and we watched TV together. It wasn't even cable. The picture quality was so bad that it was like watching ghosts in a snowstorm.

Kristina was wearing my sweatshirt, and she cuddled in my arms and soon fell asleep. I liked it that she trusted me enough to fall asleep in my arms. It made me wish I had a little sister just like her.

Maria sat next to me on the couch. She smiled at me, pointed to Gabriel and Kristina, and said, "America." Except she made the letter I sound like an *e*. "Amereeka."

I smiled. I understood that she wanted her children to be raised in America. Who could blame her for that?

I decided that's what I wanted for her and her kids too.

It's not like I didn't have money. I had plenty of money in the bank, but it was for my mission. At seventeen, though, my mission seemed a long way off.

"Jonathan, Chad, I need to ask you both something."

"What?"

"Are you guys saving for a mission?"

"Why do you want to know?" Chad asked.

"Just answer my question."

"Yeah," Chad said.

"Me, too," Jonathan admitted.

"Good. Maria doesn't have any money to pay her rent. So I was thinking we could loan her some from our mission accounts."

"Aren't there programs for people who need help with rent?" Chad asked.

"I think she's an illegal alien. If she is, she can't get government aid."

"Ask her if she is or not."

"It will take me a while to figure out how to ask that."

"We've got time."

A few minutes later, I said to Chad, "I found it."

"Ask her then."

"*Maria? Usted inmigrante ilegal?*"

"Spanish is so easy," Chad said.

"*Si,*" Maria confessed quietly. "*Inmigrante ilegal.*"

"Okay, Chad, you satisfied?" I asked. "She can't get government aid."

"You want us to pay her rent?" Chad asked.

"Yes."

"Maybe we could get the church to pay her rent," Jonathan said.

"She's not a member of the church."

"So why do we have to do it?"

"We don't *have* to do it. But the thing is, if we don't, she'll get kicked out of this place, and Gabriel and Kristina won't even have a place to sleep."

"Okay, that wouldn't be good, but why is this our problem?" Chad asked.

"We're the only friends Maria and her kids have here."

"Where's her husband? He's the one who should be paying the rent," Chad said. "Ask her where her husband is."

I threw the dictionary at him. "You do it."

"I don't need no stinking dictionary," Chad said. "Maria, husband-o, where-o?"

She shrugged her shoulders.

I got up and grabbed the dictionary from the kitchen table and returned to the sofa. After a few minutes I asked. "*Usted casado?*"

"Si."

After looking two more words in the dictionary, I asked, "*Dónde marido?*"

"*Mexico,*" she said, except it sounded like May-he-co.

"I got this one, Bro," Chad said. "Her husband is in Mexico."

Maria went to the calendar, circled a date that was two weeks ago, looked something up in the dictionary, and said something that sounded a little like our word deported,.

"He was deported?" Chad asked.

"_Sí._"

She looked up two more words. "Return soon."

"He's coming back soon," Chad proudly explained to me.

That made me so mad. "She said it in English, okay? You don't have to translate English for me."

"Hey, I can't help myself. It's a gift. Pick any language you want, and I'll translate for you."

"Maybe she plans on working until he gets back," I said. I looked up the word for work, and then I pointed to her and asked, "_Trabajo?_"

"_Sí. Trabajo._" She looked up some words and then said, "Clean house . . . your."

"She means she wants to clean your house," Chad said.

She pointed to all three of us.

"_All_ our houses," Chad said.

"If that's going to happen, we'll need to talk to our moms," Jonathan said.

"We can't do that," I said.

"Why not?"

"They'll say no. At least mine will," I said. "My dad is dead set against hiring illegal aliens. Like even with the men who come to fertilize our lawn. He goes out and makes them show him their green cards."

"Maybe she ought to just go back to Mexico then," Chad said.

"I'm sure she'll pay us back after she gets a job," I said.

"Where's she going to get a job?"

"I don't know, Chad! What do you want me to do, plan out her whole life? Look, all we have to do is pay one month's rent!"

"And how much is that?"

I sighed. "Four hundred dollars."

Chad stood up. "You're out of your mind if you think I'm going to help with that!" He was on his way out of the house when little Kristina ran to him and threw her arms around his legs.

Chad stopped, looked down at her face, picked her up in his arms, and then returned to us and sat down again. "Jonathan, what do you think?" he asked.

"I think we should help her."

Chad thought about it for a while and then patted Kristina on the back. "Okay, I'll put in a hundred dollars but that's all I'm doing."

"I can do a hundred, too," Jonathan said.

I turned to Maria, pointed first to Chad, then to Jonathan, and then to me and said, "*Dinero para casa.*" I pretended to be handing her something.

I had to do it a couple of times before she finally understood.

"No, no," she said, shaking her head vigorously.

"You want a translation, Cowboy Dan?" Chad asked. "It means, no, no."

I grabbed the dictionary and looked up the word for *and*, which is *y* but is pronounced like it was an *e*, then pointed to her kids. "*Para Gabriel y Maria. America.*"

She shook her head then left the room, crying.

"Way to go, Cowboy! You just insulted her in Spanish, didn't you?" Chad complained.

"No."

"I think you did. Besides, how would you know if you didn't?"

"You heard what I said to her."

"Well, it must have been bad. Is *para*, like a swear word in Spanish?"

"I don't think so."

"So why's she crying?" Chad asked.

"How should I know?"

Kristina and Gabriel followed their mom into the bedroom.

"Well, you've really done it this time, Cowboy," Chad said.

"What do we do now?" Jonathan asked.

"Maybe we should bring someone over here who doesn't go around insulting people in Spanish," Chad said. "That'd be a big improvement over Cowboy Dan here."

"Yeah, well, you're no help at all." I complained to Chad.

"Look, I know what happened," Chad said. "She was offended that we offered to pay her rent. I knew it was a dumb idea. Let's just go now. We've done enough damage for one day."

Chad was halfway out the door when Maria and the children came out of the bedroom. Little Kristina looked up at me with her hands outstretched. I picked her up. She threw her arms around my neck and kissed me on the cheek. Gabriel went over to Jonathan and hugged him around the waist. He knelt down and picked him up. When Chad came back into the room, Kristina ran over to him, so he picked her up too.

Maria took my hand in her hands, and with tears in her eyes said, "*Gracias.*"

"I think she's thanking us that we're going to pay her rent," Chad said.

"Yeah, I think you're probably right."

We waved on our way out the door and left.

"When our folks find out what we've done, we're all going to be in so much trouble," Chad said.

"Maybe they won't find out," I said. "Like if her husband comes back right away or if Maria gets a good job and can pay us back before our folks know what happened."

"Maybe so," Chad said.

"It doesn't matter," Jonathan said.

"Why doesn't it matter?"

"Because it's the right thing to do."

"That's what I think, too," I said.

Even so, I knew my parents would be disappointed when they found out.

This would be the first time I'd gone against their will.

But, as it turned out, it wouldn't be the last.

Chapter Three

That night I woke up at four in the morning and couldn't get back to sleep.

The money in my bank account was for my mission. It had come from my grandfather on my mom's side. When I was just three years old, my grandfather found out he had cancer and was going to die. One of his requests was that some of his money be given to his grandsons for their missions, and to his granddaughters for college. It was one of the last things he had asked for, and here I was, going against his wishes for me.

It wasn't that I wouldn't have the money to go on a mission. I knew I would. For one thing, my folks had been saving money for my mission for a long time, but I didn't have access to that money. Doing what I was about to do might make it look like I didn't even care about the last wishes of my dying grandfather.

I couldn't make something that was wrong seem right, no matter how hard I tried.

I won't do it, I thought.

That seemed to work for a while, until I thought about Gabriel and Kristina without a place to stay or else the three of them having to go back to Mexico.

I wasn't sure why Maria wanted her children to be raised in America. Mexico had always seemed like a nice place. For one thing, I've always liked their food. But I decided there must be a reason why she wanted them to grow up here. Maybe sometime she'd tell me.

I kept going back and forth in my mind about the money, but then a little before five in the morning, I worked it out in my mind. We'd loan her the money, but we'd tell her she had to listen to the missionaries. That way the money would actually be used for missionary work, like my grandfather had wanted.

That idea felt good, and I fell asleep after that. The next thing I remember is hearing the doorbell ring and my mom answering the door.

"Is Cowboy Dan up? We talked about going sledding this morning."

I swear, Chad's voice could carry a city block.

I jumped out of bed and threw on some clothes. "I'm up! I'll just be a minute."

"Please come in," my mom said to Chad and Jonathan.

"You were sleeping?" Chad asked when I came down the stairs. "How can you sleep so late?"

I hurried to get my shoes and socks on.

"What are you talking about, Chad?" said Jonathan. "You were sleeping, too, when I came to get you."

"Yeah, but I've got a good excuse. I was watching movies with my brother until two in the morning. Let me guess, Jonathan, you've already practiced your violin, right?"

He shrugged. "I like to get it out of the way."

"We could run it over with the sled and that would get it out of the way for keeps," Chad teased.

Just as we were about to leave, I remembered I needed to have my card for the savings account. "I'll be right back. I forgot something."

"What did you forget?" Chad asked.

"A handkerchief," I said.

"That's what sleeves are for," Chad said.

My mom had learned to keep a smile frozen on her face around Chad.

"I'll be right back," I said.

It took me a few minutes, but I finally found the deposit book for the account in my top drawer. Before going back downstairs, I also grabbed a handkerchief.

After I got down, I blew my nose on it just to prove I needed it.

"This is going to be so much fun, watching you blow your nose all morning," Chad said.

We were already out on the front sidewalk when my mom opened the front door and called after us, "Don't forget your sled."

"Oh, yeah. I forgot. Thanks."

I went into the garage, found my sled, and pulled it to the front of the house. "Only one sled between the three of you?" she asked.

"We're going to get Chad and Jonathan's sled now," I said.

So, of course, we actually had to do that.

A girl named Ashley rode past us in a car. She was with her folks, and they pulled over and stopped. Ashley rolled down the car window. "You guys going sledding?" she asked, in a sing-song voice. "You want to come snow-boarding with us? We've got plenty of room."

That made me mad because we didn't have the money to go snow-boarding. "No thanks!" I answered back. "Snow-boarding is for really mature people, like you, Ashley. We're just kids at heart."

She gave me a strange look, and they drove off.

"And people wonder why no girl will talk to me," Chad said. "It's totally because of you two clowns."

"What are you saying? That if you weren't with us all the time, girls would like you?" I asked.

"That's right."

"Yeah, sure, you've got what it takes to impress a girl," I said. "Girls are so impressed with guys who can belch the loudest."

It took us a while to walk to my bank, and when we arrived we agreed Chad and Jonathan would wait outside. We didn't want anyone wondering why I was withdrawing so much money.

Inside, as I waited in line, I was nervous. I'd never withdrawn money out of a bank account. I worried that they'd ask me why I was doing it, or if they'd maybe say they had to call my parents for their approval.

I also worried my mom and dad would come into the bank and ask me what I was doing. Or almost as bad, that a member of our ward would see me and then tell my mom or dad they'd seen me at the bank.

I told myself to be cool and not say any more than absolutely necessary. It was my money, and I didn't have to account to anyone for what I did with it.

"May I help you?" the teller asked.

"I would like to withdraw two hundred dollars from this account," I said, pushing the account book toward her.

"Taking advantage of all the after-Christmas bargains, right?" she asked with a smile.

"Yes, that's right."

"How would you like it?" she asked.

I was stumped. "What?" I asked, my voice cracking.

"Would you like it in tens, twenties, or a combination?"

"Uh, twenties."

A moment later she slapped each bill on the counter as she counted it out. And then she slid the money over to me.

I turned to leave.

"Wait," she called out after me.

I imagined her saying, *Isn't this the money that your grandfather gave you just before he died of cancer? Isn't this money supposed to be for your mission?* I froze, thinking she'd caught me and was going to call my folks.

"You forgot your receipt," she said, handing me a small piece of paper. She smiled. "Don't spend it all in one place."

I had no idea what that meant but nodded and quickly left the bank.

"You got the money? I got the stuff if you got the money," Chad said, making it sound like we were doing a drug deal.

I shrugged as though taking money out of my account was something I did all the time. "Yeah, sure, no problem."

On the way to the bank where Jonathan had his account, he began to freak out. He was even more conscientious than me. "You think we'll ever get our money back?" he asked.

"I think we probably will," I said.

"I'm not sure I should do this. I mean, this is supposed to be for my mission."

"We're not going on a mission for a couple of years. We'll get jobs and make up for it," I said.

"Personally, I think it's a dumb idea," Chad said. "I mean why are *we* the ones who have to bail this woman out? Do we know her? No, we do not. Can we even understand her? No, we cannot. Is she our aunt or older sister? No, she is not. Did she even ask us to help her? No, she did not. So why are we doing this?"

"Because of Gabriel and Kristina," I answered.

Chad thought about it. "Yeah, well, they are cute kids."

"You think the Three Wise Men wondered if they were ever going to get their gold back?" I asked. "No, it was a gift. And this is our gift. That's it, pure and simple."

When we got to Jonathan's bank, he tried to weasel out of it, but we shamed him into going along with our plan.

He was almost in tears when he came out of the bank.

"What happened?" I asked.

"When the woman asked me what I was going to do with the money, I lied."

"Everyone lies," Chad said. "I lie every day. I think most people do, actually."

"What did you tell her?" I asked.

"I told her I was going to buy a new TV for my mom because our old one broke and my dad is out of work. She got tears in her eyes and patted my hand when she gave me the money. I felt like such a jerk."

"That's pure genius!" Chad said. "I'm going to use that, too!"

"I feel sick," Jonathan said.

"I did, too," I admitted. "But don't worry, it goes away."

Chad had no problem. He walked in and withdrew the money. Not only that, he came out with six cookies. "They were on the counter and there was a sign that said, 'Help yourself.' So I cleaned them out."

"Did the woman ask you what you were going to use the money for?" Jonathan asked.

"Yeah, she did. I told her what you said. It worked great."

Chad ate three of the cookies and then offered us each one. I took one but Jonathan refused. "I'm not hungry."

Chad to the rescue. "Look, Johnny B, if you're going to be like this every time you go against what your folks say, you're going to have a tortured life. You got to get used to messing up so it doesn't bother you anymore. Look at me, do you see me worrying? No, you don't. I've disappointed my folks so many times, I don't even think about it anymore. They're used to it, too, so it all works out."

"Not all of us want to be like you," Jonathan said.

"Oh, yeah, I forgot. You're such a noble person. We all look up to you . . . except of course for the fact that I'm taller than you."

I tried to make Jonathan feel better. "Some day we'll probably look back on this as our best Christmas ever. You know why? Because we gave of ourselves to help a stranger."

"And that stranger will take our money and leave town and never even try to pay us back," Chad said, slapping Jonathan on the back. "Cowboy Dan is right. Look on the bright side."

When we knocked on Maria's door, we made the mistake of leaving our sleds in sight. She opened the door, saw our sleds, and called to the children. They came to the door and got excited and hurried to get ready to go sledding. I noticed that Gabriel put on my jacket and that Kristina was wearing my hoodie. That made me feel good.

"We need to talk to Maria," I said to Chad and Jonathan.

"I don't want to go sledding," Jonathan said.

"I'll take them," Chad said. "We'll slide down the little hill in front of the house."

And then they left.

We could hear the kids squealing with delight and Chad roaring.

I wanted to say, "We need to talk," but after checking in the dictionary, the best I could come up with was to say, "*Hablar.*" Without the *h* of course.

She nodded, and we sat down at her kitchen table.

I set the money in front of her on the table.

When she didn't pick it up, I thought she had forgotten what we said we would do, so I went to her calendar and pointed to the date she'd shown us when the rent was due. "*Dinero para casa,*" I explained.

She reached over and touched the money as if it were sacred.

After a minute with the dictionary, she said, "No understand."

"How do you say Merry Christmas in Spanish?" I asked Jonathan."

"*Feliz Navidad,*" he said. "I sang a song called that in seventh grade."

I repeated back what Jonathan had said.

Maria began to cry and went into the bathroom. When she came back into the kitchen, she was wiping her cheek with a strip of toilet paper.

I can't believe she doesn't even have tissues, I thought.

She patted Jonathan's and my hand and kept saying, over and over again, "*Gracias, gracias.*"

This is the way the Christmas season should be, I thought.

And then she slowly counted out the money, laying each of the twenty dollar bills back on the table. And then she took a deep breath, shook her head and slid the money back over to us.

"*Tengo que trabajar,*" she said.

"I think that means she needs to work," Jonathan said.

"What's that got to do with anything?" I asked.

"I don't know," he said.

We handed her the dictionary, and she began silently paging through it. We could hear the children laughing. I looked out the window. Chad was pulling both kids on his sled, not down the little hill on the front lawn, but up and down the street.

It took several minutes for Maria to find what she wanted to say. Finally she read what she had written. "I work for mothers. I clean." She pointed to us, which I took to mean she wanted to work for the money.

I got a sick feeling in my gut. There was no way my dad was going to let my mom hire an illegal alien.

I shook my head and looked up one word. "*Imposible.*" I wanted to tell her why, but it seemed too difficult to explain.

"Tengo que trabajar," she said again.

"She needs to work," Jonathan said.

"Yeah, I know."

"*Necesito comprar comida.*"

Jonathan looked up two words. "Okay, I got it. She needs money to buy food."

"Why's she telling us that?" I asked. "We're not stopping her from getting a job."

"*No comprende,*" I said. I'd heard someone say that in a movie.

She used the dictionary again and then said, "No papers."

I was confused. "She can't afford to take the newspaper?" I asked Jonathan.

Jonathan was puzzled too. "Papers . . . job. Papers to get a job. What could that be?"

We arrived at the answer at the same time. "She doesn't have a social security card," Jonathan said.

"Well, tell her to get one," I said.

She picked up the dictionary, paged through it again, and finally said, "*Ex-pen-seeve*." She wrote down the number 500 and then added, "dollar."

"Social security cards don't cost money," I said.

"They do if you're not a citizen," Jonathan said.

"The government shouldn't charge that much to people who just got here," I said.

"It's not the government. They're not real cards. They just look like real ones."

"So what's she saying?" I asked Jonathan.

"If she can't get a social security card, she can't get a job. And if she can't get a job, there's no point in staying here. She might as well go home. So if she's going to go back to Mexico, there's no reason for us to pay her next month's rent."

I sighed. "So, it's not just the rent? We also have to come up with five hundred dollars so she can buy a fake social security card, is that it?"

Jonathan shook his head. "I can't help with that. It's too much money."

"Go ask Chad to come back in. You pull the kids on the sled for a while," I said.

A minute later Chad came in. Even though it was cold outside, he was sweating. He wiped his nose on the sleeve of his coat and sat down. "What's up?"

"We need another five hundred dollars so Maria can buy a social security card."

"Forget it. I'm done."

"She'll have to go back to Mexico if she doesn't get the card."

"Look, I like the kids and everything, but the way it's starting to look to me, this is never going to end. I'll tell Jonathan to come back in."

Chad left.

I couldn't look at Maria. I felt bad we couldn't help her. But more than that, I felt bad that nobody wanted to help her.

It's one thing to hear people say, "We ought to send them all back to where they came from." But it's a lot different when you know someone like Maria and Gabriel and Kristina. How could I blame Maria and her husband for wanting their kids to have a better life? If I were Kristina and Gabriel's dad, and I couldn't give them the kind of opportunities they needed to be happy, I'd do the same thing.

So the way it stood, no one was going to help Maria. Not the government. Not the church. Nobody. So why is this the land of the free and the home of the brave?

None of it made any sense to me. My great-great-grandfather came to America from Scotland. My great-great-grandmother on my mom's side came here from Sweden. Why was that okay, but this wasn't?

I suddenly knew what I was going to do and it made me sad. I was going to go against what my grandfather had wanted for me. I hoped if he heard about it in heaven, he'd understand.

I stood up and said, "I'll be back."

I thought about translating it, but it would have taken too long, and I had to do this right away before I thought about it very much.

Outside, I told Chad and Jonathan I was going to the bank again, but I'd be back soon.

"What are you going to do?" Chad asked. "Give her another five hundred dollars?"

I nodded and walked away.

"That's crazy, Cowboy! Don't do it!" Chad called out after me. But I just kept walking.

At the bank I tried not to think about what I was doing. I just did it, like before, with a different teller, and nothing happened.

On my way back, though, I kept thinking about how much my grandfather loved missionary work. I had been told that he went on one mission when he was young, and another with my grandmother when they were old, and they were planning on going on a second mission when he got cancer and eventually died.

I had withdrawn seven hundred dollars of my mission fund in one day. I hoped my grandfather in the spirit world would not be told about this because I could imagine he'd be very disappointed in me.

On my way back, when I was still a block away from the house, I saw Chad pulling Kristina and Gabriel down the street toward me. Chad was running as fast as he could. The children were screaming with delight, and Chad was shouting like he was trying to kill them. *Those kids would be a lot safer in Mexico, away from Chad,* I thought.

One thought did come into my mind, though, that gave me some peace of mind. I decided I was definitely going to ask Maria to listen to the missionaries, so that way, the money could be used a little bit for missionary work.

Chad and the kids came to meet me. They were all talking at the same time.

I gave a high five to Gabriel and Kristina, and we started back up the street toward their house.

"I'm going to put a requirement on the money we give Maria," I told Chad. "She can't get the money unless she listens to the missionaries."

"So you're like paying her to join the Church? I like that! Maybe that's what I'll do when I'm on my mission."

"I'm not paying her to join the Church!" I said.

"You tell her if she wants the money, she has to listen to the missionaries. That sure looks like paying her to me."

Chad had ruined my peace of mind.

"That's not what it is."

"Hey, don't get me wrong. I like the idea. Really, if you think about it, this is like something I would have dreamed up."

He couldn't have said anything to me that would be more depressing.

A minute later I was sitting at the kitchen table again with Maria. The money I'd left on the table was still there. I pulled the five hundred dollars I'd just withdrawn out of my pocket and slid it across the table to her.

"For papers," I said.

She counted the money, looked up at me, and shook her head. "No."

"You can pay me back a little at a time—after you get a job."

I looked up the Spanish word for loan. "Préstamo."

"*Gracias.*" And then she shook her head.

She said something that had the words *madre* and *padre* in it, so I figured she might be asking if my mom and dad approved of me doing this.

"*Sí.*" I then added, "*Feliz Navidad.*" I wanted her to believe our family did this every year for Christmas. What I finally came up with after searching through the dictionary was, "*Cada año.*"

"*Why?*" she asked after going to the dictionary again.

"Jesus," I answered.

She nodded.

"Also, I want you to learn about what we believe," I said.

She looked puzzled.

"I want you to listen to our missionaries," I explained.

"*Misioneros?*" she asked.

"*Sí.*"

She knelt down and began to pray. I felt like an idiot sitting there watching her pray, not understanding a word she was saying.

I think though, looking back on it now, she was thanking God for answering her prayers.

When she finished praying, she got up, pointed to heaven, and scooped the money from off the table and put it into the pocket of her dress.

She now had seven hundred dollars of my money, a hundred dollars of Jonathan's money, and a hundred dollars of Chad's money.

On the way home, I didn't want to talk to Chad and Jonathan about what had just happened.

I didn't feel heroic or noble. Mostly I felt numb and a little ashamed.

Chapter Four

O n Sunday in priesthood meeting, the bishop gave the sister missionaries a few minutes to talk about missionary work.

"Whose responsibility is missionary work in the ward?" Sister Davis asked.

Silence. We all knew the answer but there was no way anyone was going to say it.

"Ours?" the high priest group leader finally said.

"That's right," Sister Davis said. She was full of enthusiasm. Her companion, Sister Rodriguez, was Hispanic. She didn't say much, but she had a great smile and was way better looking than Sister Davis.

"How can you interest your friends, coworkers, and neighbors in learning more about the Church?" Sister Davis asked.

Chad leaned over and whispered to me, "Just tell 'em you'll give 'em nine hundred dollars if they'll meet with the missionaries."

I quickly glanced around to make sure nobody else had heard him. Apparently nobody had.

In two minutes Sister Davis gave ten suggestions of things we could do to interest our friends and neighbors in the Church. And then she added, "If you have anyone we can visit, let us know. We'll be in the hall after you separate for classes. Oh, sorry, I mean quorums."

When we were dismissed, I hung back and waited for everyone to leave.

And then I entered the hall. Sister Davis and her companion were standing there. When Sister Davis realized everyone had gone, she lost all her perkiness. "They just need time to think about it, that's all," she said, sounding a little discouraged. "We'll stand in the hall after Priesthood and Relief Society for people who want to give us referrals."

"Okay," her companion said.

I walked toward them. They didn't pay any attention to me until I said, "I know three people you can teach, but they only speak Spanish."

"I speak Spanish," Sister Rodriguez said.

"Is this a friend from school?" Sister Davis asked.

"No. A few days before Christmas the youth delivered boxes of food to needy people in our ward, Two of my friends and me took our box to the wrong house. That's how we met this Mexican woman and her two kids."

"What's her name?"

"Maria Sanchez," I said. "And her kids' names are Gabriel and Kristina. Her husband is in Mexico now. He was here for a while, but they caught him and sent him back."

"Do you think she would be willing to let us teach her?" Sister Davis asked.

"Yeah, she will. I already asked her, and she said yes."

"You talked to her? Do you speak Spanish?" Sister Rodriguez asked.

"No, but my friend Jonathan has a Spanish-English dictionary."

"Can you give us her address?" Sister Davis asked.

"I'd rather go with you. Can we do that after church? It's just a few blocks from here."

Sister Davis looked at her appointment book. "Yes, that would work out for us, wouldn't it, Sister Rodriguez?"

Sister Davis was in charge, that was plain to see. I figured she only asked the question to make her companion feel as though they were a team.

"Yes," Sister Rodriguez said.

But then I thought about all the hassle it would be to explain everything to my mom and dad after church and decided it would be easier to do it right away. "Actually, we could go now, if you want."

"You should be in priesthood and we should be in Relief Society," Sister Davis said.

"Let's just go," Sister Rodriguez said. "That's why we came on a mission, isn't it?"

Sister Davis thought about it. "All right. I suppose just this once it will be okay."

And so we left the church and started walking. Sister Davis made me promise to go home and read the priesthood lesson so I wouldn't miss it. I said I would, but I knew I'd never do it.

Sister Davis was the kind of person that when you walk with them, you know they want to walk faster but they don't because they think you'd never be able to keep up.

Actually, I felt a little sorry for Sister Davis. She was the conscientious one, the one who could never relax, who was always wondering if they were doing enough. She was also the one I figured most people would have a hard time feeling close to.

Sister Rodriguez was not only beautiful, but she also seemed at peace with the world. She even asked me about my family. She asked how many brothers and sisters I had. I told her I had two older brothers who had been out of the house since I was twelve.

She told me she had three brothers and two sisters. She was the third child. Her older brother had just returned home from a mission.

My guess was that Sister Davis would never ask how many brothers and sisters I had unless they were not members of the Church and there was a chance she could teach and baptize them.

Sister Davis could have worn contacts but she didn't. She could have worn warm colors but instead chose clothes the color of a cloudy day. She looked at her watch. "How much farther is it?" she asked.

"Just a block. Why?"

"It's just that we should be back by the time priesthood is over, in case someone has thought of someone we can teach."

"They can call us," Sister Rodriguez said.

Being with Sister Davis depressed me. Mainly because I was so much like her. When Chad and Jonathan and I were together, nobody paid any attention to me. Chad was bigger than life. I could never compete with him in anything. Sports came easy to him. Making friends with girls came even easier. Every girl in school thought she was his best friend.

And then there was Jonathan. He was better looking than either Chad or me. Because his mom had been born in Guatemala, he always looked tan. He had a great smile too. Girls fell in love with him, but he didn't seem to notice it. Also, he treated every girl with respect, even ones that weren't that great looking.

Jonathan was like the definition of nice guy. I'd never seen him do anything mean to anyone. In that sense he was more like a girl. Well, actually, that's not true either because I've seen plenty of girls do mean things to other girls. I'm not sure how to explain it. He just seemed to care about people. It was like a part of who he was.

And then there was me. I was the one who did both the even and odd math problems, even though only the even ones were assigned, because I wanted to make sure I was going about it the right way, and the answers for the odd problems were in the book. I was only popular just before class, when people needed to find out how I'd done the homework.

It wasn't that girls didn't like me. It was more that they didn't notice me. Like at dances. When I walked up to a girl to ask her to dance, I would always notice her eyes darting back and forth to see if someone better than me might be on his way, too, so she wouldn't have to waste her time on me.

Because I felt sorry for Sister Davis, I said, "Sister Davis, that was real good what you said in priesthood meeting about missionary work. I just want to say, you're doing a great job!"

She stopped and turned around and looked at me. I knew she didn't know what to say. Like I wouldn't have known, either. You can give me a job to do, just don't give me praise.

"Thank you," she said, still off balance.

A few minutes later we stood at the door. I knocked.

When Maria came to the door, she smiled warmly and called out my name. Gabriel and Kristina ran to the door and into my arms. I knelt down to give them one big giant hug.

Maria invited us in. I introduced Sister Davis and Sister Rodriguez to Maria, Gabriel and Kristina. They were about to eat and invited us to eat with them. Sister Davis and I would have politely declined, thinking they had so little food we didn't want to put them out. But Sister Rodriguez quickly said, "Si, gracias."

They only had two extra chairs so I let the sisters sit at the table while I ate on the couch. We had beans and rice. I never knew something like that could taste so good.

Sister Rodriguez and Maria talked the whole time. All Sister Davis and I could do was look like we understood everything.

A few minutes later, Sister Rodriguez turned to me. "Maria wants you to know that she got a job at the meat packing plant. She likes it very much. She wanted me to thank you for helping her get the job."

"I didn't do anything."

Maria pulled out her social security card and proudly showed it off and then gestured with her hand to me, like I was the one who made it happen.

Sister Rodriguez had a surprised look on her face.

Sister Davis looked at her watch. "We need to begin if we're going to teach."

I was relieved when Maria put her social security card back in her purse.

Sister Rodriguez started to teach Maria and her kids.

I kept glancing at Sister Davis to see how she was doing. To me she looked a little disappointed. I figured I knew why. It was because she'd always been the one in charge, the one who took the lead, and now she couldn't do that. She probably felt this was a waste of time, not because it was, but because she wasn't in charge.

I knew how she felt. It was like me watching Chad live a charmed life. I worked harder, but good things came naturally to him. Most teachers didn't expect much from him, so when he put out even a little effort, they were quick to praise him.

Gabriel and Kristina sat on my lap during the lesson. Once in a while Sister Rodriguez would ask the kids a question. She always praised them, whatever answer they gave.

Sister Rodriguez turned to me when we were about to leave. "They want us to come back," she said excitedly. "You, too." she said.

"Okay."

"When could you do it?" Sister Rodriguez asked.

"Next Sunday, during priesthood," I said.

"No, you should be in priesthood, and we should be in Relief Society," Sister Davis said.

"How about Wednesday night?" The reason I chose Wednesday night was because it was activity night for the youth in our ward, and I wouldn't have to explain to my mom and dad why I was gone.

We set it up for Wednesday night.

Sister Rodriguez coached Maria about how to pray, and then we all knelt down, and Maria said the prayer. She did an okay job I guess, but of course it was in Spanish so I wasn't sure what she was saying. She had to stop once because she was crying. My eyes got a little moist too, but I managed to wipe my face before the amen.

On our way back to the ward, Sister Rodriguez turned to me and said, "Maria told me that you and your friends gave her nine hundred dollars to pay for her rent and, also, to help her buy a social security card."

I laughed. "Did she tell you that?" I said it as though that was the most ridiculous thing I'd ever heard.

"Did you do that?" Sister Rodriguez asked.

I nervously cleared my throat. "Well, yeah. The three of us helped her with her rent, but, actually, I was the one who paid for her social security card."

"Social security cards don't cost anything," Sister Davis said.

"Not actual ones, but fake ones do," I said.

"Isn't that against the law?" Sister Davis asked.

"Gosh, I don't know. Is it?" I asked.

"It is." Sister Rodriguez said.

"All I know is that she needed one to get a job," I said.

"Where did you get the money?" Sister Davis asked.

"I had money in the bank. Actually, it was for my mission."

Sister Davis looked at me like this was the sin of the century. "Do your parents know about this?"

I chuckled. "Oh, yeah, sure. Actually, they were the ones who suggested it." I lied.

"I would be very surprised if that were true," Sister Davis said.

"Tell us the truth, Dan," Sister Rodriguez said.

I would never lie to Sister Rodriguez. "No, they don't know about it."

"You need to tell them," Sister Davis said, once again on the offensive.

I shook my head. "I can't do that. I'll make plenty of money this summer working. I'll put all the money back into the account." I paused. "Or maybe Maria will pay me back."

"Do you want us to talk to your parents?" Sister Davis asked. "Because we can't work with you when they have no knowledge of this."

"It's my money. I should be able to do with it whatever I want."

"Not if it's been dedicated to the work of the Lord."

"This is the work of the Lord. And it is missionary work."

"But it's not your mission. You can't let this go on without your folks knowing about it," Sister Davis said.

I knew she wouldn't get off my back until I agreed. "Sure, no problem, I'll tell 'em today," I said. "As soon as I get home from church."

"Will you promise us?" Sister Davis asked.

"Yeah, sure," I said, willing to promise anything to get her to quit hassling me.

Sister Davis smiled. "Good. We'll check with you later and make sure you've done it."

I shrugged. "Whatever."

Sister Rodriguez touched the sleeve of my coat. "Maria calls you and your friends 'my angels.'"

"Believe me, we're no angels," I said.

"She thinks you are," Sister Rodriguez said.

"That's good, I guess."

"Even so, it doesn't make it right that you did this without talking to your mom and dad first," Sister Davis said.

"Will you quit hassling me about this?" I shot back.

"He said he'll tell his parents," Sister Rodriguez said. "I am sure Dan will do what he says he will do. He is a man of honor."

That was even worse than having Sister Davis on my case. It was the first time anyone had called me a man. That part I liked, but the truth is I didn't have any intention of telling my folks everything, so saying I would and having Sister Rodriguez believe me made me feel guilty.

I knew that now I'd have to tell my mom and dad something. If I didn't, Sister Davis would do it for me. I needed to tell something but not everything. Lately that had been what I did with my mom and dad. Tell as little as possible.

The way I look at it, if you want your kid to reveal every thought and action, be a mom and get yourself a daughter.

During Sunday dinner, I decided to finish my dessert before I said anything to my mom and dad, in case they sent me to my room to think about what I'd done. I'd had that punishment before. It wasn't that bad. I just watched TV.

"Mom, today in priesthood the sister missionaries talked to all of us about sharing the gospel. That made me think about something that happened when we delivered Christmas boxes to the needy in our ward. I haven't told you this before, have I?"

"Told us what?" my mom asked.

"Well, Chad and Jonathan and me made a little mistake and delivered our box to the wrong house."

"Chad, Jonathan, and I," my mom said. She was always trying to get me to improve my English.

"Did you go back to the first house and rectify your mistake?" my dad asked. He loved to use big words.

"We tried, but the mom didn't understand English. But when we got to Jonathan's house, we called the bishop and told him about the mix-up. He said he'd take care of it."

"You boys need to be more careful when you are carrying out a ward assignment," my dad said.

"I agree. That was a dumb thing to do. It will never happen again."

"I don't understand how this relates to the missionaries coming to priesthood," my dad said.

"Well, I was just getting to that."

I sighed. This would be the tricky part, saying just enough to satisfy them but not too much.

"Well, today, the sister missionaries said if we could think of anyone that they could teach, that we should talk to them about it. So I talked to them right after the opening part of priesthood, and they were excited to hear about this woman and her two kids. The only time they could do it was then, so we walked over to her house, and they taught them."

"You missed priesthood?" my mom asked.

"Yeah, but only because this was missionary work, and there's nothing more important than missionary work."

"I'm sure missing one lesson won't hurt any," my dad said.

I had to say something about money because that was the first thing Sister Davis was going to say. "Oh, one other thing, when us guys visited her, she was out of milk and bread, so we gave her a little money to get what she needed. She said she'll pay us back though. So I guess you could say we loaned her some money."

There, that should do it, I thought.

My mom nodded and then got that look that meant she might cry, "Your grandfather would be so proud of you for being such a good missionary."

"You think?" I asked.

I was relieved it had gone so well. Okay, the part about the money for milk and bread wasn't exactly the truth, but it's all a matter of degree, right? Whether you loan somebody money for a quart of milk and a loaf of bread, or you loan them seven hundred dollars from your mission account, it's all just a matter of degree.

A few hours later Sister Davis called. My dad was giving us a spiritual message. Something about Isaiah or food storage, I can't remember which.

"Did you tell your parents about the money you loaned Maria?" she asked on the phone.

"Yeah, sure. Just a minute." I spoke as loud as I could, almost as loud as Chad. "Mom, it's Sister Davis. She wants to make sure I told you guys about us loaning money to Maria."

It was a gamble, but I gave the phone to my mom.

"Sister Davis? Oh, fine, how are you? Yes, Dan told us all about it. We're fine with it."

No use pushing my luck. "Mom, we're going to go to Maria's house Wednesday night to give her another lesson. So I need to talk to the missionaries about that."

My mom gave the phone back to me. I wandered into the kitchen. "So, did you have anything else for me tonight?" I asked Sister Davis.

She told me they'd meet us at Maria's at seven Wednesday night.

At seven-thirty that night the doorbell rang. I was in my room. My mom came to the door and knocked. I turned off the TV and opened the door.

"Jonathan's sister, Michelle, is here. She says she needs to talk to you."

Michelle had come to our back door, by the kitchen. Fortunately, my mom and dad were in the living room.

Michelle looked embarrassed. "These are for you," she said, handing me a plastic bag of cookies. "I made them for you."

"For me? Why?"

"Jonathan told me about you loaning money to . . . uh . . . Maria and her kids."

I looked around to make sure my mom or dad weren't listening in. "Please don't tell anyone about it, okay?" I said.

"I won't."

I opened the bag and looked at the cookies. "Thanks, Michelle. That's very nice of you. They look really good."

She paused, looked down at the floor, and then, almost in a whisper, said, "You're, like, my hero."

We made eye contact for just a second, and I could see in her eyes that she meant it. I really was her hero. *That's just not right*, I thought. *I shouldn't be anyone's hero.*

"Thanks," I said.

"If you ever need someone to talk to, call me," she said.

"I will. Thanks," I said.

"Well, I'd better go," she said.

"Wait. Why am I your hero? That doesn't make sense."

"Because you gave away all your money to help someone."

"Oh." I sighed. "The only trouble is that it was the money I was saving for my mission."

"I know. You'll make that money back." She sighed. "And if you don't, I'll give you some of my money."

"You'd do that?"

"For you I would."

I didn't know what to make of this. I wanted to tell her she was wrong about me. But I didn't because a part of me wanted it to be true. I wanted to be her hero. Actually, I'd be happy being anybody's hero.

"Thank you for coming over. And for the cookies. And . . . for what you said. That means a lot to me. It really does."

"Don't worry. I won't make a pest of myself. That's what Jonathan said when I told him what I wanted to do. I didn't tell my mom and dad either. They would say I'm too young for this."

"Too young to bring cookies?"

"No. Too young to have a crush on a senior."

Whoa, that was awkward. I didn't feel the same way because to me she'd always been Jonathan's little sister.

I knew enough to be kind, though. "I am totally honored you'd have a crush on me," I said.

She nodded. "Thanks. Well, I'd better be going."

"Okay, thanks for the cookies. I'll enjoy them."

She nodded again and left.

I dumped the cookies in the front kangaroo pocket of my hoodie and started upstairs.

"What was that about?" my mom asked.

"Michelle made me some cookies."

"What for?"

"I guess she made too many and needed to get rid of some of them."

"Where are they?" my mom asked.

"I put them in the pocket of my sweatshirt. You want some?"

"Not if it's in that sweatshirt," my mom said.

"I see what you mean," I said. Lately I had found that to be a very useful expression. It sounds as though you've learned something from the experience.

I went upstairs, dumped the cookies on my desk and started eating them. They tasted good.

I thought about the responsibility I had now to be a better person, so as not to disappoint Michelle.

I decided I needed to pray more, and read the scriptures for seminary, and call my home teaching companion and not just hope he'd forget about it and we wouldn't have to go that month.

I knelt down and prayed and asked God to forgive me for giving away all the money that my grandfather had given me for my mission. I wasn't clear in my mind if this was my money or if it was God's money because it was supposed to be used for my mission. If it was my money, then it wasn't really sinning. But if it was God's money, then it would be like stealing from God, which is way worse than just having bad judgement.

I prayed that Father in Heaven would help me get the money back before my mom and dad found out, but I wasn't sure that was the right thing to pray for.

I didn't pray, though, to be forgiven for not telling my mom and dad the complete truth about the money, because I knew if I asked that and somehow God told me to tell them everything, I still wouldn't do it.

Some things it's best not to pray about.

Chapter Five

onday, after school, Jonathan and I did homework together at his house.

Chad never joined us. He always had more important things to do. He usually just copied our work on the way to school the next day.

We were working on the kitchen table. Michelle came in to get an apple. Now that she had a crush on me, I wondered if this time would be any different from all the other times we'd seen each other.

She seemed the same. But I wasn't. On her way out, I said, "You look totally awesome today, Michelle."

Her eyes darted first from me and then to Jonathan. She started to blush. "Thanks," she said under her breath and then quickly escaped.

Jonathan looked at me. "What was that all about?"

"I just thought she looked good today, that's all."

He shook his head. "This is so weird."

"Let's just finish up here."

He shook his head. "My sister? She's only fourteen."

"What did I do that's so wrong? I told her she looked good. Is that like the crime of the century?"

It was then I realized that having a girl with a crush on me was much more complicated than I had ever imagined. Of course it had never happened before. Girls don't usually go for math and science geeks.

On Wednesday night, Jonathan, Chad, and I walked to Maria's house. We got there a little late. Sister Davis and Sister Rodriguez were already there.

Kristina and Gabriel ran to Chad. He picked Gabriel up and then pretended he weighed so much he couldn't hold him. He dropped him and caught him just before he reached the floor. Kristina begged him to do it to her. So he did. And then Gabriel again and then Kristina again.

Sister Davis cleared her throat and said we should probably get started.

Sister Davis turned to Maria and very slowly said something in Spanish.

I figured she'd been practicing on it. It sounded a little weird, but Maria responded enthusiastically. "Very good. Very good."

Sister Rodriguez taught the rest of the lesson. It went very well, I guess. Maria must have given all the right answers because Sister Rodriguez smiled a lot and said *bueno*, which means good in Spanish.

The sister missionaries invited Maria to go to the Spanish branch on Sunday. She said she would like that, then turned to the three of us and said something in Spanish.

"Maria wants the three of you to come too," Sister Rodriguez said.

"We'll be there!" Chad said enthusiastically.

I stared at Chad. He usually wasn't that excited about church.

"I'm supposed to give a talk in church. Now I have an excuse," he explained.

Unfortunately for Chad, the Spanish branch met at one o'clock. Our ward met at nine, so Chad would still have to give his talk. But, even so, he still wanted to go.

Sister Rodriguez also invited Maria to go to a Spanish branch social on Friday night. She asked us to go, too.

"Will they have good food?" Chad asked.

"I'm sure they will," Sister Davis said.

Chad was so predictable. "We'll definitely be there."

Then Maria asked Gabriel to say the prayer, and Sister Rodriguez helped him.

After the prayer we had flan. Chad had his doubts. He leaned over and whispered in my ear. "You think this is safe? It looks like something that somebody's hurled."

"I'll try it."

I took a spoonful and then said to him, "It's not too bad, but if you want, I'll eat yours."

He tried some. He liked it, too.

We talked for a while and then Sister Davis looked at her watch and said they needed to be going. Sister Rodriguez looked bummed they had to go.

"Who else are you teaching tonight?" I asked.

Sister Davis looked annoyed at my question. "We need to get prepared for tomorrow."

I looked at Sister Rodriguez. She didn't say anything, but I could tell she wanted to stay.

"Sister Davis, did you have a good time tonight?" I asked.

She seemed confused why I would ask the question.

"Yes, I did. I love teaching the gospel."

"Does it bother you that you can't speak Spanish, and that Sister Rodriguez is doing all the teaching?"

She looked down and cleared her throat, so I knew I'd nailed how she was feeling. And then she looked up at me. "I'm always glad to have Sister Rodriguez as my companion, especially now."

I worried I'd hurt her feelings or made her mad. "You and I are a lot alike," I said.

"What do you mean?"

"That's the way I would be if I were you."

"What way is that?"

"Wanting to do everything and getting frustrated when you can't."

Sister Davis does this thing when she's mad. It's like her lips disappear.

The sisters left so Sister Davis could make us believe they were so busy all the time. My friends and I stayed for a while and played Chutes and Ladders with Gabriel and Maria. But just before starting another game, Maria asked to talk to me.

We sat at her kitchen table while Jonathan and Chad continued playing with the kids in the living room.

We had to use the dictionary again. She started. "Me . . . paid . . . Friday."

"Very good." And then I added, "*Bueno,*" just so she'd know I could learn another language too.

She had to look up some more words.

"Need . . . food . . . family . . . ahora . . . You help?"

I looked up the word ahora. It means now. But don't let the *h* fool you. They just throw that in to make sure Gringos like me will have a hard time learning Spanish.

As soon as I realized where this was going, I got a sinking feeling in my stomach. She was asking for more money.

"*Que mucho?*" I asked, which I hoped meant how much. Oh, the *q* is another trick for people like me, too. It's pronounced like a *k*. And forget the *u* and the *e* too.

She got a piece of paper and wrote down the number 20.

I asked, "Twenty?"

"Si. Twenty." And then she added, "Veinte."

Chad was now on all fours, being a bear, chasing the kids around the living room and even into the kitchen. They loved it of course and ran screaming by us, followed closely by a growling Chad.

Maria looked at me with a worried expression on her face. I think she saw how hard this was getting for me.

I took a deep breath and nodded and looked up the word for tomorrow.

"Manana?" I pronounced it as if it rhymed with banana.

She smiled and pronounced it as though there was a y in the word. "Mun-yauna."

I later learned that it's another trap for people like me. The little wiggly line above the n means you have to throw in a y there somewhere.

She nodded and smiled. "Gracias."

I was beginning to feel like I was being taken advantage of, and suddenly I didn't want to be there anymore. "Chad, Jonathan, let's go. I need to get home."

"You want to be the bear?" Chad asked. "My knees are killing me."

"No, I just want to go home. I'm tired."

I was the last one out the door. "Mañana?" I asked.

"Yes," she said in English

I was so tired of looking things up in the dictionary. "*Trabajo* . . . uh . . . *cinco* o'clock?" I asked.

"Si."

"*Buenas nachos!*" I called out.

She broke into a silly grin and waved.

The kids insisted on hugging us at the door. Especially Chad. Not so much me.

On the way home, Jonathan informed me that instead of saying good night, I had actually said "Good nachos!"

Chad couldn't stop laughing, and then added, "And may you have a good taco, too!"

That night I lay in bed and worried. I wondered if my grandfather on my mom's side, even though he was dead, somehow knew what I'd been doing with his money. I was sure he'd be disappointed in me. That was what my mom and dad always said when I messed up. "We're just very disappointed in you, Daniel." Oh, yeah, they also call me by my official name when they're disappointed in me.

Actually I was a little disappointed in myself, too.

Except for one thing. The question that always came to my mind was, "If I don't help Maria and Gabriel and Kristina, who will?"

"It doesn't have to be you," my dad would have said. "These people can always go back to Mexico where they belong."

I need to tell you more about my dad. When he was growing up, his grandparents had a small grocery store in New Mexico. Sometimes people who were having a hard time would buy groceries on credit until things got better. Some of them were from Mexico. Eventually his grandparents were in so much debt they had to sell the store. That didn't help how my dad felt about Mexicans.

Also, to make matters worse, my dad was an accountant working for Patient Account Services at our local hospital. He complained a lot about illegal aliens coming to the emergency room for treatment, setting up a payment plan but then never paying what they owed.

Those two things were probably responsible for his bad attitude and where his wanting to "send all the illegal aliens back" came from. I don't want you to think he was a racist. In fact, he often said, "I'm not a racist, but. . . "

But how great can it be there in Mexico for them if they're willing to risk their lives crossing the border to get here?

One thing I knew for certain. Maria loves her kids and wants them to have a chance to have a future where they can get an education and a decent job.

I tried to pray, but I didn't get very far because sometimes I picture God to be just like my dad. But I did ask Father in Heaven to tell my grandfather on my mom's side that I loved him, even though he might not think I did because of what I'd done with all the money he'd given me for my mission.

The next morning, as I lay in bed, I tried to analyze in my mind exactly how my folks would find out that I'd given away most of the money in my mission account. I knew they sometimes got statements from the bank showing the interest the money had earned. I knew that because one time they showed me my money had earned four dollars and thirty-six cents. They seemed quite excited about that, and I guess they were hoping I'd be excited too. I remember thinking, So what?

The next time the bank sends a record of my account, that's when my mom and dad will find out how little money is in the account now, I thought. *But what if there isn't any money in the account? What if I don't even have that account anymore? Then the bank won't send a letter, and they'll never find out.*

Suddenly I had a plan. I'd close out the account, and then as I earned more money, I'd keep it at home until I had the right amount and then I'd open up a new account. And they wouldn't even know what had happened.

It was a brilliant plan. *That's what I'll do*, I thought.

The next day I went to the bank.

"May I help you?" the woman behind the counter asked.

"I would like to close my account," I said, handing her the account number.

"I see," she said. "Have you been unhappy with our service here?"

"Oh, no, your service here has been real good. It's just that the only reason I had the account was to buy a used snowmobile, and now that I've paid for it, I have no more use for the account." Telling lies was actually getting quite easy for me.

"Of course," she said.

"Just one thing. You won't be sending any more statements to me, will you?"

"We usually send a statement verifying that the account is closed. Would you prefer that we didn't?"

"Yes, I would, actually."

"We can do that."

"That would be good."

Her eyebrows shot up and I knew she was suspicious. "Do your parents know what you're doing with this account?" she asked.

"Oh, yeah, sure. In fact my mom sent me here to do this. You can call her at work if you want. I've got the number here somewhere."

The truth is my mom didn't work outside the home. I started going through my pockets as though I was trying to find the number.

People hardly ever take you up on offers like that, especially in a bank with impatient customers behind you in line, and you're having a hard time finding the number. They assume if you tell them to check out what you've said, it's got to be true.

"No, that's okay. I trust you," she said. "You have a balance of forty-seven dollars and twelve cents."

"That sounds about right."

"What would you like that in?"

"Tens."

She did something on her computer and then counted it all out for me to see that she was giving me the right amount.

As I left the bank, at first I felt excited that my plan had worked, but then I remembered my grandfather, how much he wanted me to serve a mission. What I'd just done felt as though, at the cemetery on the day of his funeral with everybody watching, I'd gone up and spit on his casket.

He had worked all his life as a janitor in a grade school. He and Grandma were never rich. They lived in a small house with two small bedrooms and a tiny yard that was almost all garden. And in the summer he worked mornings at the school, getting everything ready for when school started in the fall, but in the afternoon, he worked in his garden.

So the several hundred dollars he gave me for my mission would be like thousands of dollars for someone who'd had a better paying job.

Maria only needed twenty dollars, but I had forty-seven dollars and twelve cents. At first I thought about getting something for myself, but after a while I decided against it because the money was sacred in a way, and I didn't want to be selfish with it. So I decided to give it all to Maria so she could get something nice for her kids. Except I'd keep the twelve cents.

Even though I was trying to help someone, I didn't feel right about what was happening. I mean, whatever good feelings I had were overshadowed by the lies I'd told. I also knew that my dad would think I was being conned by Maria. And I could see why he might think that. Of course, if she paid me back then it would be a good thing, but if she didn't then anyone who knew about it would tell me I was an idiot for giving a stranger seven hundred and forty-seven dollars.

There was only one person I could talk to about this. It wasn't Chad, and it wasn't Jonathan. Strangely enough, it was Michelle, Jonathan's sister. I knew she'd understand.

When I rang the doorbell, Jonathan's mom came to the door. She smiled and let me in and told me she'd get Jonathan. She told me he'd been cleaning his room.

He came to the front door and asked me if I'd help him clean his room. I said yes and followed him upstairs.

Once we were in his room, I said, "Actually, I want to talk to Michelle."

He looked at me strangely. "Why?"

"I need to ask her something. Is she home?"

"She's cleaning her room too."

"Could I go in there and talk to her?"

He shrugged his shoulders. "Yeah, sure, I guess."

"Would you tell her I'm here and ask if I can come talk to her?"

He nodded. "Okay." He let out a big sigh as he headed for Michelle's room.

A minute later he came back and told me she said it was okay.

I went into her room and closed the door because I didn't want her mom to know I was talking to Michelle.

"Is everything okay?" she asked.

"No, not really. I took out all my money from my mission account today."

"Why?"

"It's kind of a long story, but that Mexican lady we met needed money for groceries. After I leave here, I'm going to her place and giving it all to her."

"Oh."

"But the good news is she gets paid Friday."

"Does that mean she'll pay you back?"

"I don't know. She never said she would. At least I won't be giving her any more money because there's nothing left."

"Oh."

I closed my eyes. "Could you tell me again that I'm your hero?"

"You are . . . my one and only hero."

"Thanks. I don't feel like anybody's hero. I feel like I've gone against what my grandfather wanted me to do with that money. He was the one who put most of the money into that account. It was supposed to be for my mission. "

Just then her mother opened the door. I could tell by the look on her face that she was shocked seeing me there. "Daniel, what are you doing in my daughter's bedroom with the door closed?"

"Nothing," I said, feeling suddenly very embarrassed.

"We were just talking," Michelle said.

"Michelle, you are not to have a boy in your room, and certainly not with the door closed. Dan, I want you to leave this house now."

It finally came to me what she was worried about. "But, it's not like that! I just wanted to talk to her."

"Please leave this house."

I had to make her understand. "No! I won't leave until you give me a chance to explain! This is not fair!"

That made her mad. "I beg your pardon? Do you want me to call my husband . . . or the police?"

"I would never do anything, you know, like uh, bad to Michelle."

"Then why did you two have the door closed?"

"I needed to tell her something. The reason I would never do anything to hurt Michelle is . . . well . . . because she thinks of me as her hero."

"Hero or not, you have no business being alone with her in her bedroom. My gosh, Daniel, she's only fourteen."

"I'm almost fifteen!" Michelle protested.

"I know how old she is," I said.

"Then why are you confiding in her?"

I sighed. I decided it would be better to be thought of as foolish with money than to have her suspect me of being sick and twisted.

"Okay, I'll tell you what the problem is. Before Christmas, when Jonathan and Chad and I were delivering the Christmas box for the bishop, we took it to the wrong house. We tried to get it back but the woman didn't understand English, so we left the box with her. Well, later, we found out she needed money to pay her rent, so we all chipped in to help her. And then she had some other expenses, and I helped her with that. I had some money in the bank. And well, today, I withdrew out all the rest of my money for her."

"How much money did you have in the bank?"

"About seven hundred and fifty dollars."

"Oh, Dan," she said, sitting down on the bed next to Michelle.

"But, you know what? It's okay. Maria's getting paid Friday, so she'll pay me back. Well, not all of it on Friday, I guess, but I'm pretty sure that within a month she'll pay it all back, and everything will be back to the way it was. So the reason I wanted to talk to Michelle was because one time she told me I was her hero, and, well, I don't feel much like a hero today. I feel like an idiot for taking money my grandfather gave me for my mission. So that's why I wanted to talk to

Michelle. It wasn't about, you know, bad things. I would never do anything bad to her like what you must be worrying about."

Michelle's mom thought about it for a while and then said, "Michelle, is that the truth?"

"Yes."

I needed to add one more thing. "I think my grandfather must be really disappointed in me. He's dead now, so I can't find out for sure." I didn't want to do it, but suddenly I felt as though I was going to cry.

She called Jonathan into the room. "Jonathan, did you put in any of your mission money to help this Maria?"

He gulped and gave me an accusing look. "Yes."

"How much?"

"A hundred dollars."

"You did this without even asking for permission?"

"Yes."

"I'm very disappointed in you."

"Sorry." He left.

"Are you going to tell my folks?" I asked.

"Well, first of all, you were in my daughter's bedroom with the door closed. I think your parents should know about that, don't you?"

I folded my arms over my stomach and lowered my head and rocked back and forth and hoped I wouldn't get sick on Michelle's carpet.

"Mom, that is so unfair," Michelle said. "It's not like that."

Her mom continued. "I also think I should tell your mom and dad that you've withdrawn all the money from your mission bank account and given it to someone you don't even know."

"I'd rather have you tell them I was in Michelle's room."

"Why's that?"

"Because they'll know me being in here with Michelle was just because I wasn't thinking. I'm not like that. Michelle knows it, Jonathan knows it, and my folks know it."

"Why don't you want your folks to know about the money?"

"Because what I've done with it is like spitting into my grandfather's grave."

"Then why did you do it?"

"Maria needed some money for her family. And I wanted to help her. That's all."

"Her rent was eight hundred dollars?" Jonathan's mom asked.

"No, she needed other things."

"What other things?"

"You know, soap, towels, food, warmer coats." I knew it would be a mistake to tell her I'd also given money to Maria so she could buy a fake social security card.

Her mom looked at Jonathan and me. "Do you boys know that some people make their living lying so people will give them money?"

"We went to her house by mistake. And she never asked us for money," I said.

"Well, I guess we'll just have to see if she'll make an effort to pay back your generosity."

"So you won't tell my mom and dad?" I asked.

"Not about the money, at least for a little while. But there's still the fact of you being in Michelle's room alone with the door closed."

Michelle shook her head. "Mom, he was in here about two minutes, and all he did while he was here was rock back and forth like he's doing now. He looked like he was going to cry."

"I wasn't going to cry!" I said.

"Sorry," she said.

"What are your feelings for Dan?" her mom asked Michelle.

She blushed, looked away, and then said softly, "I don't know any other boy in school who would help a mother and her two kids when the mother doesn't even speak English. I think that he must be a very good person to do that. That's why I told him he's my hero."

Their mom looked at Michelle and then at me, sighed, and said,

"I see." She sighed again, and then said, "Daniel?"

"Yes."

"Being a hero is not always an easy thing. Please don't ever disappoint Michelle or me."

"I won't. I promise."

"Very well, then. It goes against my better judgment, but I won't say anything about this to your mom or dad."

"Thank you."

"But you must stay out of her bedroom. And, Michelle, you are not to go into his bedroom . . . ever. Do you understand?"

"I won't, okay? Why do you have to keep talking about this?"

When I left Michelle's room, I didn't want to be with Jonathan anymore. I worried that maybe he and I wouldn't be as good of friends as we used to be. Like, he'd always wonder why I was coming to his house, to see him or his younger sister, who didn't seem old enough really to have boys my age noticing her.

"Well, I'll see you around," I said to Jonathan.

"Yeah, sure."

Just before I got to the door, he said, "That was so weird."

"I know."

"You and my sister?" he said, shaking his head.

"It's not like that."

"I would have no respect for you if it was."

"I know. Me, either. I'll see you in school tomorrow."

"Yeah, sure."

"Can I come by and pick you up tomorrow morning?" I asked. We usually walked to school. I would go to Jonathan's house and then we would walk together to Chad's place, wake him up and fix him toast with peanut butter while he dressed, and then the three of us would walk the rest of the way.

"I guess so."

After I left Jonathan's place, I hurried to Maria's house and gave her the money. I stayed at the door and didn't go in because I didn't want to hear about it if she needed more money from me.

After I'd left, she must have noticed I'd given her forty-seven dollars instead of the twenty dollars she'd asked for. She opened the door as I was walking away *"Esto es damasiado dinero!"*

I had no idea what that meant. *"Para Gabriel y Kristina!"* I said with a big smile.

She smiled at me. "Thank you much."

I waved and hurried home.

The next morning I didn't even go into Jonathan's house when I came by for him in the morning. I just stayed outside and practiced trying to hit one of their trees with a snowball.

On Friday Chad asked us if we were going to the Spanish branch party that night. Jonathan and I weren't too excited about it but he wanted to go so we said we would.

It was too far to walk, but Jonathan's mom said she'd take us. When she came by and honked, Chad and I ran out and got in the backseat with Jonathan. And then I noticed Michelle was there, too. Sitting up front.

I couldn't figure it out. What was this, some kind of a test to make sure I wouldn't say hello to her?

"Hello, Daniel," their mom said.

"Hello."

"Yeah, hi," Michelle said.

"Hi."

I looked over at Jonathan for an explanation.

"We're all going," he said quietly. "My dad's out of town tonight. My mom wanted to see what the Spanish branch is like."

"Oh."

"My mom is Hispanic, you know," he said.

"Oh, okay."

We parked in front of where Maria lived, and we all went to the door.

When she opened the door, Chad called out, "Buenos nachos!" He turned to me and laughed. "Cowboy Dan, you want to wish her good nachos, too?"

Gabriel and Kristina ran to Chad, and he picked them up one at a time and pretended he was about to drop them. They squealed with laughter. It was obvious that they loved Chad. But who didn't?

Jonathan's mom spoke Spanish. I think she introduced herself to Maria, and then we all went out to the minivan and piled in.

Jonathan's mom asked Michelle to sit in the third seat, between Jonathan and me. Chad sat in the middle seat with Gabriel and Kristina, and Maria sat in the front passenger seat.

While we were driving, the two women talked in Spanish. They talked so fast, I couldn't understand anything they were saying, but they were laughing like they were old friends.

Chad pretended to be a bear and made threatening growls at the kids. They giggled and screamed.

I stared straight ahead, afraid to say anything for fear of making Michelle's mom mad at me.

"Aren't you going to talk to me?" Michelle asked softly.

"I can't decide," I said.

"Go ahead if you want. My mom doesn't think you're a pervert anymore," she said.

Chad leaned forward. "Michelle, why did you say that to Cowboy Dan?"

"No reason."

"Has he been hitting on you?"

"No! Of course not."

"Well, if he does, let me know, so I can tell all his friends in his honors math class. They'll be both shocked and pleasantly surprised."

I wiped the sweat from my forehead and made a rule to never talk to a girl again. It only leads to trouble.

The Spanish branch met on the upstairs floor over a furniture store warehouse. The branch had a big sign taped on the window on the second floor indicating it was The Church of Jesus Christ of Latter-day Saints. And once you climbed the stairs and went inside the large room it looked and felt a little like being in a ward cultural hall.

The party was in the biggest room. Folding chairs had been lined up around the walls, and there were some tables set up with food on them. I could tell it was used as the chapel on Sunday because of the wooden plaque listing the hymn numbers.

Crepe paper streamers had been hung from the center of the ceiling and went out like spokes on a wheel. Strings supported the crepe paper. Also on the strings were lots of colorful balloons.

At first people were just standing around talking, but after a few minutes, President Rivera, the branch president, welcomed us and called on someone to say the prayer. The brother who prayed did so in Spanish, but we could tell when it was over when everyone said, "Amen." Then it was time to get in line for food. They must have been expecting a big crowd because there was so much food! They even had extra food in the room next door.

While we were waiting in line, President Rivera stopped to say hello and to welcome us. He spoke both English and Spanish. He wasn't very old. I mean not like my bishop. Maybe in his thirties, I guess. He was very friendly and introduced us to his wife and kids. Sister Rivera was beautiful. In fact most of the women were. Maybe it's because of their dark skin and brown hair and brown eyes. People like me, that is white, in the winter we look like the living dead—pasty and sickly looking. But not these people. They always look great.

Everyone was so friendly. I watched Maria as people came up and greeted her. Most of the woman hugged her and kissed her on the cheek. They did that to Jonathan's mom, too.

For me this was like just having arrived in heaven. Or at least it was the way I hoped heaven would be like.

The food was great and there was plenty of it. And Chad didn't pass up any of it. At first I didn't take any guacamole. But when Chad told me how good it was, I tried it, and went back for more. It was especially good on tortilla chips.

After we'd eaten, they had a dance. But the music wasn't like the music we have for stake youth dances. This had more of a beat to it. Chad didn't hesitate but got out there right away with Gabriel and Maria and danced with them. He kept faking falling down and getting up again. Then all the kids got into the act. Ten or so kids at a time— laughing and giggling as Chad kept pretending to trip and fall down.

After a while, Michelle came over to me. "Dance with me."

I shook my head. "I don't think so."

"It's okay with my mom. I asked her. It doesn't mean anything. It just means we'll be dancing instead of sitting around watching everyone else have fun."

"I'd rather not."

That made her mad. "Get over yourself! Okay, one time I said you were my hero, but don't let that get to you. You're not that much fun to be with. Not like Chad. He's always fun. You're always worrying about your stupid homework. See, I could never like a guy like that. So don't worry that I'm going to end up liking you, okay? You're my hero now, but so what? I'm sure you'll disappoint me eventually, and then I'll totally ignore you for the rest of my life."

"You think?" I asked, suddenly full of hope for our non-future.

"Yeah, for sure."

I gave a big sigh of relief. "Thanks."

"So dance with me now, okay?"

I nodded, and we went out onto the floor. I led her to the side of the room, as far away as possible from her mother.

They were doing a dance I'd never seen before, so at first I just stood next to Michelle and watched her dance, but then little by little

I tried to do what everyone else was doing.

At first Chad was dancing with like twenty kids. But then he saw a girl more our age and, for the children's benefit, went over to her to ask her to dance but pretended to trip and fell down in front of her.

She, along with everyone else, was laughing. He got up and put out his hand, and she took it and they started dancing. All the younger kids circled around them and did their version of the dance too.

The girl was the most beautiful girl I'd ever seen. She was tall for a girl, but not as tall as me. She had long dark brown hair that went way past her shoulders. It was parted in the middle and swayed back and forth as she danced. She also had a great laugh. It wasn't like some girls, who cover their mouths when they laugh. Oh, no, she apparently found Chad very funny and let it all come out.

I was standing there with Michelle, staring at the girl Chad was dancing with. "Hold me, Dan. I won't break," Michelle said to me, having to almost shout to break my concentration.

I held Michelle but at arm's length, like I was afraid I'd get germs from her if we danced too close.

"Closer, okay? This feels like I'm dancing with myself."

"What about your mom? She might not like us dancing close."

"Don't worry. She'll be okay with it. All I want is that we be as close as everyone else who's dancing."

The girl Chad was dancing with looked very happy to be with him. He danced twice with her and then took her back to the chairs and went to a grandmother type and put out his hand to dance with her. She at first looked surprised but then smiled and got up and they danced. Everyone seemed very pleased that he was dancing with her.

After a few minutes, Jonathan came over to me and asked if he could dance with his sister. Of course I let him.

I asked Jonathan's mom if she wanted to dance. I thought she would say no because that's what my mom would have said, but she didn't. She got up and we danced. It was a little bit awkward, but we somehow managed. It was even kind of fun.

When the song ended, we went back to the side where Michelle was sitting. Jonathan had disappeared.

"Are you having a good time?" Jonathan and Michelle's mom asked.

"I love this!" she said. "This is way better than our ward. These people know how to have fun. I want to come here all the time."

"I agree," her mom said. "And I would, except for one thing."

"What's that?" Michelle asked.

"I'm in the Relief Society presidency, remember?"

"This branch has their meetings in the afternoon, so you could still come," I said.

"I suppose. And I will, sometimes. It's good for me to be speaking Spanish again." She looked around. "Do you know where Jonathan is?"

"No, not really. If you want, I'll go find him."

"It's okay. I was just wondering." She put her hand on my arm. "Thank you, Dan, for asking me to dance. I can see why you're Michelle's hero. You look out for people."

I was glad she was no longer worried that I was some kind of pervert.

I found Jonathan in the other room that had food in it. He had a plate of food in his hand, but he wasn't eating any of it. Instead, he was talking to an old man, or rather the man was lecturing him. "You need to learn Spanish. You need to not walk away from your heritage. You need to lift up your people, not pretend they don't exist. The Anglo culture doesn't need you, but we do."

Jonathan was just nodding his head. I couldn't tell if he agreed with the old man or was just being polite.

"Your mom asked me to find you," I said. "She wants to know why you're not dancing."

Chad had abandoned the beautiful girl our age and was now dancing with Michelle.

"Go ask that girl," I told Jonathan, pointing to the girl Chad had been dancing with.

"No."

"Why not? She's gorgeous."

"Why would she want to dance with me?" Jonathan asked.

"Because she's not dancing. She loves to dance. Go ask her."

"You ask her first," he said, "and then I will."

I was feeling a little macho. "Okay, I'll show you how it's done." I walked over to the girl. "Hi. You want to dance?"

She smiled. "Yes, I do! Thanks!"

We started to dance. Her eyes were dark brown and she had long eyelashes. She looked so good that I could hardly stand to look at her.

"How long have you been in America?" I asked.

She scowled.

I didn't know if she'd understood my question. "The reason I ask is because you speak very good English," I said.

"I was in one of your classes last year," she said.

"You were?"

"Yes. You never talked to me."

Oops. I needed to explain. "Yeah, that sounds about right. If a girl is really pretty, I totally ignore her. So that explains it. It wasn't, like, racial, okay?"

"Why do you ignore pretty girls?" she asked.

"Most girls don't want to talk to me. So this way everybody's happy."

"I would have liked to talk to you."

"Why?"

"Because you were the smartest guy in the class."

I sighed. "Well, yeah, I was. I always am." She was so beautiful that it made me nervous. I needed to think of something else to say. "Uh, are you a member of the Church?"

She pulled back a little and kind of squinted at me. "What If I weren't? Would you stop dancing with me?"

"No, I would still dance with you. I like dancing with you."

"I wish I could say the same," she said. And then she put her hand to her mouth and laughed. "Sorry, I didn't mean it the way it sounded. It's just that you dance, well, like a Gringo."

"That's because I am."

"I know that."

"Teach me to dance like they do in Mexico."

"I can't."

"Why not?"

"Because I'm not from Mexico."

"Where are you from?"

"I was born in Texas, but my mom and dad were born in Ecuador."

"Oh." I felt like an idiot. "Name one difference between Mexico and Ecuador."

"For one thing, we don't eat Mexican food. We eat Ecuadorian food."

"Oh, yeah, sure, like instead of beans and rice, you eat rice and beans, right?"

She laughed again. "Forget what I said about you being smart."

I shrugged. "Okay, but look, I'm willing to learn. That's what smart people do, you know."

"Sometime I will cook you some of our food, and then you'll know."

"What's your name?"

"DeAnna. It's spelled D-e-capital A-n-n-a."

"That doesn't sound like an . . . Ecuador-type name."

"My parents wanted me to have an American name, so I'd fit in better."

"What's your last name?" I asked.

"Ortiz. What's your name?"

"Dan."

"Are you the one Chad calls Cowboy?"

"Yes."

"You don't look like a cowboy. Why does he call you that?"

"Because my last name is Winchester. And there used to be a gun called the Winchester rifle. They say it helped tame the Western part of the United States."

"Oh."

"Could you show me how to dance?" I asked.

"Yes. Rock back and forth to the music and watch me."

"That I can do."

She broke away from me and danced. I'd never seen a girl who could swivel her hips and move her body like that. People stopped dancing to watch her. All I did was stand there, swaying back and forth—and feeling stupid.

"Now you do it," she said.

I tried to imitate her, but all it did was make everyone laugh.

Chad swaggered over to us. "Hey, let me show you how it's done, Cowboy."

He did a thing like he was a bullfighter. She caught on and pretended to be a bull.

Stamping his feet like a flamenco dancer, Chad started calling out every Spanish phrase he'd picked up in all the movies he watched. "*Ràpido!* Hasta la vista, baby! *Buenos Nachos!*"

It was pure Chad, and everyone was laughing, including DeAnna.

I walked slowly back to where Jonathan, Michelle, and her mom were standing.

"Good job, Cowboy Dan!" Michelle said. "That's the most normal I've ever seen you."

"Thanks," I said, turning to watch Chad and DeAnna putting on a show for everyone.

"I should have asked her to dance when I had the chance," Jonathan said sadly.

"You can still do it."

"No, she'll be with Chad the rest of the night."

"Just go over there and ask," I said.

But just as Jonathan stood up, President Rivera had someone turn off the music and asked for everyone's attention. He thanked us all for coming to the party, speaking first in Spanish and then translating what he'd said into English for us.

He told us the branch was like a family and said they needed everyone in the family and that he missed those who weren't coming on Sundays. He said he loved us all, then gave his testimony and asked someone to say the closing prayer.

I couldn't believe the party was over. The time had raced by.

Chad brought DeAnna over to Jonathan and me. "We're all going to start eating lunch together at school. Is that okay with everyone?"

Jonathan and I both enthusiastically said yes.

On the way home, Maria said she'd come to the Spanish branch with us on Sunday, and Jonathan's mom said she'd pick her up.

When we got home, I went to my parents' room and told them I was home. My mom asked me if I had had a good time.

"Yeah, I did. We all did, including Maria."

"Who's Maria?" my dad asked.

My dad never seemed to remember anything. "A nonmember that Chad and Jonathan and I met when we were delivering food boxes to the needy for Christmas. She has two kids. She's from Mexico, and her husband is going to come here soon."

"Legally?"

"I don't know. She's going to go to church Sunday to the Spanish branch. It meets in the afternoon. The missionaries think it would be good if Chad and Jonathan and I go, too."

"I don't see anything wrong with that. Do you, Michael?" my mom asked.

My dad's name is Michael , and he doesn't like people to call him Mike. That tells you a lot about how I was brought up, right?

"I guess one time wouldn't do any harm," my dad said.

"Anything else you want to tell us?" my mom asked.

"No, that's about it."

I could have told them I'd just met the most beautiful girl in the world and that we'd danced together and that she'd teased me. But, no, that was enough communication with my mom and dad for one night. My new motto for dealing with my parents had become, *Give them enough so they don't worry what you're hiding from them.*

I had a hard time getting to sleep that night. I kept thinking about DeAnna Ortiz. I figured Chad and Jonathan were probably doing the same thing, but that was all right. This beautiful, charming girl was going to be eating lunch with us at school. That had never happened to us before. Of course, I'd seen girls eating with guys at school before, but they were always popular guys. Not guys like Chad, Jonathan, and me.

The last thought I had before falling to sleep was, *This is going to be so good!*

Chapter Six

When I woke up on Sunday and entered the kitchen, my mom reminded me that it was fast Sunday, which meant no breakfast and possibly no lunch either, or at least not one my mom would fix. She would take a nap after church for a few hours. I didn't think that was fair because of course it's easier to fast when you're not awake.

Our testimony meeting was like usual. There were two babies blessed. I liked the second blessing the most because the baby screamed like crazy the whole time and the father practically had to shout.

Later in the meeting one of the new moms got up and talked about the miracle of birth and thanked people for bringing in all the delicious casseroles, cakes and cookies. That didn't make fasting any easier.

After church, Chad, Jonathan, and I got a ride home with Jonathan's mom and Michelle. Jonathan's mom fixed us lunch, and then we jumped into the car and made our way to where the Hispanic branch met. On the way, we picked up Maria, Gabriel, and Kristina. Maria looked great in her Sunday dress, and the children were both scrubbed up and looking good. People in the branch seemed happy to see us, especially those who had been at the party on Friday night. The women who'd met Jonathan's mom and Maria at the dance greeted each of them with a hug and a kiss on the cheek. That still seemed a little strange to me, but I later learned that was a custom among the Hispanic members—the women kissing each other as a greeting.

This is so cool, I thought. *It's like we're a family.*

When DeAnna saw us, she also came to greet Chad, Jonathan, and me.

"You're supposed to give us a big hug, then kiss us on the cheek," Chad teased her.

She laughed. "Nice try. But would you like me to sit with you and translate?"

"If you sit next to me and forget about these two clowns with me, I don't care if you translate or not," Chad said.

She smiled. "If you don't care about the translation then, I'll sit between Jonathan and Dan and translate for them."

"Man, I walked into that one, didn't I?" Chad said.

"Yes, you did. Jonathan and Dan, let me sit between you."

We took our seats. Michelle, Jonathan, DeAnna, me, Chad, on one row. Behind us were Jonathan's mom, Maria and her children, and Sister Rodriguez and Sister Davis.

The meeting started about five minutes late. That was okay with me because everyone was having such a good time talking to each other.

President Rivera got up to conduct. As he spoke, DeAnna translated. She spoke in a whisper, and I leaned close to her so I could hear every word, or at least that would have been my excuse if she'd called me on it. But she didn't. She smelled good too.

At first I was so focused on the fact that I was sitting next to a gorgeous girl that it was hard to pay much attention to anything else. However, I did get more focused when we sang the sacrament song. DeAnna helped me pronounce the words in Spanish. Also, I noticed the sacrament prayers sounded better in Spanish.

After the sacrament, it was time for testimonies.

A woman got up. "This is Sister Martinez," DeAnna whispered. As this gray-haired woman was speaking, I forgot about DeAnna and paid attention to her testimony. She told us she cared for a woman who was in her eighties. But about a month ago the woman had become sick, and her doctor said she might die. So Sister Martinez called her family and asked them to pray for this woman.

The old lady began to get better. In fact, she started feeling so well she told Sister Martinez that she wasn't sure she even needed her help anymore. But of course she did.

"God hears our prayers," DeAnna said to us in translation.

Then a young woman holding a baby got up. "This is Janet," DeAnna said.

Janet began to talk.

I leaned closer to DeAnna, partly because I wanted to understand what Janet was saying. "In her native country Janet would often ride a bus that traveled through a mountainous area. One day, the bus came, but Janet had a strong impression that she should not get on the bus. So she decided to wait for the next bus, even though it would not come for several hours."

Janet stopped speaking to calm her baby, and then began again.

When DeAnna didn't say anything, I looked at her. Her eyes were brimming with tears, so I knew what Janet was saying must be good.

"Sorry," DeAnna finally whispered. "As she rode the next bus, they came to an area where there were ambulances and police cars. She found out that the bus she would have been on went off the road and down a steep mountain. Most everyone was killed. If she hadn't listened to the Spirit, she would have probably died."

Janet sat down.

Then one of the counselors in the branch presidency got up.

"This is Brother Flores," DeAnna said. "That's his wife sitting over there."

She motioned to a mother with four young children, the oldest being maybe eight or nine.

DeAnna summarized Brother Flores's testimony. "Their youngest recently got very sick, so he and President Rivera gave him a blessing. He was better the next day."

"We don't have much money," DeAnna said, suddenly switching to what Brother Flores was saying instead of just summarizing. "So when our kids get sick, we pray and give them blessings. Heavenly Father hears our prayers and honors the priesthood we hold and gives us the blessing we need. We are very grateful. I know this church is true. In the name of Jesus Christ, amen."

And so it went, one after another. For us Gringo boys, it was like we'd never attended a testimony meeting in our lives. Suddenly the gospel became real to us.

Sister Rodriguez, my favorite missionary, bore her testimony. She spoke first in Spanish and then in English for our benefit. "After I submitted my papers, I wasn't worried where I'd go. I always had it in mind that I would go to Central or South America because I had grown up speaking Spanish in my family. So when my call came to serve an English-speaking mission in Utah, I was very sad and wondered if they hadn't made a mistake."

When she spoke in Spanish. I found a word or two I understood. That somehow made me feel good.

A minute or two later, Sister Rodriguez switched back to English. "I asked my father what I should do. He told me this was a call from the Lord and that if I served where I was called, I would someday realize that Father in Heaven knows what He is doing."

Sister Rodriguez continued in Spanish. I turned around to look at Sister Davis to see how she was taking this. She caught me looking at her and smiled. I'm still not sure what that meant, but I think it mean she was okay with having her companion do so well. I hoped that was it.

Then Sister Rodriguez told us in English what a blessing it was for her to teach Maria and Kristina and Gabriel. And said how happy she and Sister Davis were that Maria and her family had come to church. And then she bore her testimony about the Savior and about the restoration of the gospel.

A few minutes later President Rivera looked as though he was about ready to stand up and end the meeting when Maria stood up and walked quickly to the stand.

She looked at us and started crying. She was struggling to control her tears, and one of the counselors reached to hand her a tissue. Then she began to speak.

She spoke fast, and DeAnna gave us a summary.

"She's grateful for the missionaries who are teaching her. She's grateful for the people she's met. This feels like this is her family away from home, and she loves being here."

DeAnna paused.

"Now she's talking about you guys . . . how she'd prayed and asked God to help her with Christmas. And then how you came and gave her a box of food and that you, Dan, came back that night and gave your coat and sweatshirt to her kids, and then after Christmas the three of you came with toys and games and puzzles for her kids. And how you . . . "

Maria was continuing to speak but DeAnna stopped to look at me. "You guys loaned her money for rent and food?"

I felt guilty admitting it. "Yeah, maybe, I guess."

"I can't believe you'd do that for someone you don't know very well."

"We did it for her kids. They needed a place to stay and food to eat."

I was feeling pretty good about myself while Maria continued to talk. That is, until DeAnna leaned over to me and whispered, "She just said you loaned her money so she could get papers."

I closed my eyes, knowing this was not going to be Maria's and my little secret anymore.

I nodded.

"That could get you in a lot of trouble," DeAnna whispered.

"What are they going to do, deport me?" I asked.

"No but they might send you to prison."

"Only if they find out the card is fake."

"Are you willing to go to prison for Maria and her kids?"

I shrugged. "I don't know. I haven't thought about it."

"Maybe you should."

"What can I do now? What's done is done."

"Where'd you get so much money?" DeAnna whispered.

"My mission savings account." I sighed. "It's all gone now."

"Oh my gosh, Dan, you should have talked to me first," DeAnna said.

"I didn't know you then."

"Do your folks know about this?"

"No, and they probably won't, either, because I closed the account, so they won't get any statements anymore. My plan is to earn money and save up until I have enough to open a new account."

She reached for my hand and held it. She leaned into me and softly said, "You've got a good heart, but I'm worried about you."

As soon as the meeting ended DeAnna turned to me and said, "We need to talk."

"Wouldn't you rather talk to me?" Chad asked.

"Not right now."

She got Maria and suggested the three of us go outside while Chad and Jonathan watched her kids.

Once we got outside, DeAnna spoke to Maria for a few minutes in Spanish. I could only pick up one or two words.

And then Maria went back inside the building.

"This is what I said to her," DeAnna said. "If ICE comes to the place where she works and finds out she can't speak English and yet she has a social security card, they might be suspicious."

"Maybe so."

"What I suggested is that she let me teach her English so immigration won't be suspicious if they show up someday."

"Good idea," I said. Looking for any excuse to be with DeAnna, I added, "Maybe I could come and learn Spanish too."

"I'd like that. She studied my face for a moment. "What you did was very generous."

We looked into each other's eyes. I thought this was it. True love, at last, had come to me.

Then she brought me back to reality. "But it could get you into a lot of trouble."

Sister Davis and Sister Rodriguez came over to talk to us.

"We're going to teach Maria another discussion. Would you like to join us?"

"Yes, we would," DeAnna said.

But on our way in, President Rivera asked if he could talk with me, and we went into his office. "You and your two friends helped Maria with her rent and food?"

"Yes."

"And you gave her money to buy a social security card?"

I hesitated, then admitted it.

"Do your mother and father know that you did this?" he asked.

I think I probably could have lied to him, but one time my bishop in a temple recommend interview told me that he was acting in place of the Lord, so I should be perfectly honest.

I couldn't tell for sure if this was the same thing. The question in my mind was under what circumstances can you lie to a bishop or a branch president? I decided that if you were at his house and they were serving fish, and he asked you if you liked fish, but you didn't, you could lie. That would be all right. But probably not in his office when he's acting in the role of a priesthood leader.

"Actually, no, they don't. Not yet. But I'm going to tell them."

"When are you going to tell them?"

I thought about it. "I was thinking, maybe right before I leave on my mission."

He scowled, so I knew that wasn't the answer he was looking for.

"I'll tell them right after Maria starts to repay what I gave her. You know, so they won't worry she's not going to pay me back."

"When will that be?"

"Real soon. Maybe in a week, I think."

"Have you talked to Maria about her paying you back?"

"Uh, not exactly."

"I think you should."

"Okay."

"Do you understand the social security card she got is not valid and that the federal government could go after her once they find out it's not a valid card? If she tells them you gave her the money for it, you could be in trouble also."

"I guess I never thought about that."

"That's why it's important to tell your parents."

"If I do, they'll never let me come here again. And, I have to tell you, this was so much better than my ward. I'd like to come here every week."

"I can't give you permission to do that."

"I'll go to my home ward first and then come here. So that's okay, isn't it? Especially while Maria and her kids are learning about the Church."

He thought about it. "All right."

He let me go. I wandered around the building until I found Sister Davis and Sister Rodriguez, teaching Maria and her two kids in one of the classrooms. Jonathan's mom was with her but not DeAnna or Jonathan and Chad.

I finally found them, sitting in Jonathan's mom's SUV.

When I opened the car door, DeAnna was laughing, and I knew Chad and Jonathan were entertaining her.

"You guys aren't with Maria and the missionaries?" I asked.

Chad shrugged. "We thought we'd have our own private Sunday School lesson out here."

There was no way I could match Chad when he was being his charming self.

"Okay, well I think I'll go in for Maria's lesson."

"Whatever," Chad said.

I could see Jonathan was feeling a little guilty, but I knew he didn't want to leave Chad alone with DeAnna.

I waited for him to respond, but when he didn't say he wanted to go with me, I closed the car door.

I found the classroom they were in and sat behind Maria and her kids and Jonathan's mom. In a short time, Kristina was sitting on my lap.

Sister Davis was speaking in Spanish. It was slow and a little painful to listen to, but when she was done, both Maria and Sister Rodriguez told her she'd done a good job.

I was proud of Sister Davis because she was trying so hard. I admired her for that, and wondered if I'd do the same on my mission.

"Good job, Sister Davis," I said.

She turned and scowled at me. I guess she didn't think it was right to keep getting compliments from a guy, even if the guy was five years younger than she was.

That's the way I would have been, too. I always go way overboard with trying to follow the rules. That is, except for aiding and abetting an illegal alien so she can buy a fake social security card.

Strangely enough though, I didn't feel like a criminal.

As the lesson continued, I noticed that Maria looked so much happier now than when we first met her.

That made me happy too.

On Monday at school, DeAnna ate lunch with Chad, Jonathan, and me. Having a girl like her at our table made us feel like we had status. And the amazing thing was, she acted like she enjoyed being with us. For one thing, we could make her laugh. Or at least Chad could.

With her next to me, the cafeteria food tasted better, the lighting was brighter, and it was fiesta time for us three boys. She was like a sign that said, "These guys actually know a beautiful girl who isn't even ashamed to eat with them." It was, up to then, the highlight of my high school experience.

Even after lunch it seemed to me the guys in my math class looked at me with greater respect. And some girls I passed in the hall suddenly seemed to consider me as having more worth.

Tuesday after dinner, the sister missionaries taught Maria and her kids more about the church. Since DeAnna was going to be there, Chad, Jonathan, and I showed up too.

My two friends and I had suddenly changed our focus from being a support to Maria and her kids to just trying to impress DeAnna. After the lesson Chad played with the kids, and Jonathan practiced his Spanish with DeAnna. I, unfortunately, because I'd promised President Rivera I would, asked Sister Rodriguez to help me talk with Maria about the money I'd loaned her.

"It's about the money we loaned you," I said to Sister Rodriguez for her to tell Maria. "That money is for my mission, so I need you to pay me back, when you can, that is."

After Sister Rodriguez translated what I'd said, Maria nodded and said, "*Próxima semana.*"

"Next week," Sister Rodriguez said.

"That would be great," I said, feeling much better. If she paid it all back next week, then I could open up the account again and everything would be back to normal.

On the way home Chad told us he'd asked DeAnna to the movies on Friday.

"You mean, just you and her?" I asked.

"Yeah, so?"

"I thought we had an agreement," I said.

"What are you talking about?"

"I thought we'd agreed to do everything together."

"I never agreed to anything like that," he said.

"If you start going with her, then we'll never see her."

"It's just a movie, that's all. No big deal."

I figured Jonathan would back me up, but he didn't so I asked him what he thought about it.

"It's okay."

"What, are you crazy? Why would you say that?"

He sighed. "My mom asked her to have dinner at our house after church on Sunday."

"What is wrong with you guys? Don't you see this will be the end of us being best friends?"

"You want me to choose between DeAnna and you two clowns?" Chad asked with a smirk on his face. "Sorry, but you lose on that match-up. I'll take DeAnna over you guys any day."

"Hey, you know what? Maybe I'll ask her out, too," I said.

Chad shrugged. "It's a free country. Do whatever you want."

I felt as though I'd been betrayed. But I could play that game too. That night I tried to call DeAnna several times while I did my homework but the line was always busy.

The next morning in school, at first I decided that I wouldn't sit with Chad, Jonathan, and DeAnna at lunch but then worried if I did that, DeAnna might think I didn't like her. So I joined them.

Chad sat on one side of her with Jonathan on the other and me across the table from the three of them.

It was like a contest to see who could impress her the most, but nobody could ever top Chad. He could make me laugh even when I was mad at him.

It's a little hard to describe Chad's humor. He never said much that was actually funny. He made us laugh because of his ability to imitate any of our teachers, or our principal, or anyone else. And he loved slap-stick comedy, like walking toward a wall and kicking it just before his head touched it, so it looked and sounded as though he'd hit his head on the wall.

While DeAnna was gone to get an ice cream bar, Chad turned to me. "Hey, don't worry about asking DeAnna out. I worked it out with her. You're going to take her bowling Saturday afternoon."

"You asked her out for me?"

"Yeah, sure, what are friends for?"

"That really makes me look pathetic," I said.

Chad laughed. "Hey, you are pathetic, but so what? The thing is, she's willing to go out with you."

On my way to math class, a guy who weighed about three hundred pounds stopped me. "So, who are your new amigos?" He used the word amigo like it was a swear word.

"What are you talking about?"

"You're spending a lot of time with Mexicans lately. How come?"

"You have a problem with that?" I asked.

"Yeah, I do. We got enough of them people here already."

That made me mad. I gave him a shove. "You jerk, get out of my way! I'll mingle with whoever I want to. I really don't care what you think."

Much to my surprise, he backed away from me.

In math class I tried to critique what I'd said to the guy who'd stopped me. I realized that if I'd thrown in a couple of swear words it might have been more convincing. Also, who can respect anybody who uses the word mingle? I was cursed having a dad with such a big vocabulary.

Why is it I have to completely dumb down everything I say to the morons in this school? I thought. *Well, I'm sick and tired of it.*

A few minutes later Mr. Jenkins drew a line on the board and then drew a curve that kept getting closer and closer to the line. "What's that?" he asked.

I raised my hand. "That's an asymptote," I said.

"That's right."

Ordinarily I would have been embarrassed for knowing things like that, but not anymore.

"How do you know that?" the guy next to me asked.

"Don't any of you guys read ahead in the book?" I asked.

The people around me looked at me as though I were a traitor to the cause of promoting ignorance.

You know what? I didn't care anymore.

The next day during lunch Chad asked us if we'd ever seen the movie *The Three Amigos*. Even though we'd all seen it, he described his favorite parts, imitating Chevy Chase, Steve Martin, and Martin Short perfectly. And then he said, "We ought to call ourselves The Four Amigos. What do you think? It's perfect, right? There's four of us, and we're friends. And the Spanish word for friend is amigo. So we're The Four Amigos, right?"

Whenever Chad had an idea, he got so excited it was infectious. Even though it sounded stupid, we couldn't help going along with it, and we nodded politely. That's all Chad needed. From then on, we were officially The Four Amigos.

On Friday night Chad took DeAnna out. The whole evening, I kept thinking about them. It was all I could do to finish my homework.

Then, on Saturday, I took DeAnna bowling. I figured I'd pick her up in our car, but at the last minute, my dad was called to help someone in our ward, so that was out.

I called DeAnna to cancel, but she said she only lived three blocks from the bowling alley, so if I could get to her house, we could walk.

I ended up riding my bicycle to her house.

When she saw me on the bicycle, I said, "Sorry. It was the only way I could get here."

"You don't have to apologize to me about that. I don't have a car, either."

We started walking. It was cold but at least the sun was shining.

"Can I hold your hand?" I asked.

She looked at me. "Why do you want to hold my hand?"

"Because you probably won't let me kiss you, so at least that would be something, right?"

She shook her head. "That's your answer?"

"Yeah, why?"

"It's not what a girl wants to hear."

"Why's that?"

"Well, for one thing, do you even like me, or is this just a contest between you and Chad to see who can get the farthest with me?"

I groaned. "Did he kiss you last night?"

"I don't see that's any of your business."

"That means he did, right?"

"It means I don't want to answer your question. Why does everything to a guy have to be a contest?"

This was not going well. "Sorry."

"Okay."

After walking in silence for a while, she turned to me. "The truth is I like you more than any guy I've ever known."

"More than Chad?"

"Why are you asking me that? Are you going to brag to him about this?"

"No."

"You will. You're a guy. I'm not saying any more about this, okay?"

A couple of minutes later, she reached for my hand, and suddenly we were holding hands as we walked. I'd learned my lesson, though.

I didn't say anything about it. I knew whatever I said, she'd get mad and pull away from me.

We walked in silence until we were almost at the bowling alley. Then she turned to me and said, "I pray for you every night."

"You do?"

"Yes."

I wanted to know if she prayed for Chad and Jonathan, too, but I wasn't going to ask.

"Thank you," I said.

At first I wanted to bowl better than her, but then I figured out that is what most guys would do so I decided not to worry about who won.

She beat me. I tried to act like I didn't care, but the truth is I did. I knew Chad would ask who won, and when I admitted DeAnna had beat me, he would ask me how I could let a girl beat me.

I didn't have an answer for that question except to admit she was better at bowling than I was. But to Chad that excuse would be totally unacceptable.

On our second game, I think she started trying to lose to me, which made me try even harder to do badly. I think it wasn't much fun for either of us.

On our walk home, I asked, "You're going to start going with Chad, aren't you? Well, you know what, I don't blame you. He's a lot of fun to be with."

"Are you still worrying about him? Why does he have to be here with us even when he's not? I like you, I like Chad, I like Jonathan."

"But you like Chad most of all, don't you?"

"You know what? I'm not going out with just one of you ever again."

"You're going to eat with Jonathan after church tomorrow though, right?"

"Yes I am, but that's because his mom asked me."

When we got to her door, she didn't even ask me in.

"Thank you for taking me bowling," she said with an edge to her voice.

"You're welcome," I said.

When I got home, I went inside and answered "Okay," when my mom asked me how it had been bowling with DeAnna and then went up to my room and finished my homework. Both the even and the odd problems.

Chapter Seven

The next week was the best week I ever had in high school. On Tuesday night, DeAnna and I went to Maria's house for English lessons, with DeAnna doing the teaching. Mostly what we did was walk through the house. DeAnna would point at, say, a glass. First she'd say the word in Spanish for my benefit, like for example plátano for banana, and then she'd say the English word. And so it would go as we walked around the house naming other items along the way.

The third or fourth time we made the tour it became a yellow banana. And then the next time it was, "I want to eat a yellow banana."

To Gabriel and Kristina this was like a game, and they loved it.

After an hour, Maria fed us guacamole with nachos. It was fun for me being with them, especially without Chad there to steal the show.

Maria told us how excited she was that her husband Eduardo was about to cross the border and join up with her and their kids. She said it first to DeAnna in Spanish and then DeAnna told me in English.

Maria told us that she'd talked to Eduardo about the Church and that he was interested. She wanted Sister Rodriguez and Sister Davis to teach him once he made it home.

After the lesson, I walked DeAnna home. I didn't hold her hand, but I thought about it.

Something I said made DeAnna laugh once. Or at least chuckle. Certainly nothing as spectacular as what Chad would have done but it made me feel good that I could at least do that.

At her house, just before she went inside, DeAnna gave me a hug. Not a long hug but at least it was a hug, so that's got to count for something.

That should have made me happy, and it did for like a couple of minutes, but then I thought, *If she's doing that to me, what is she doing to Chad? He's ten times better around a girl than I am.*

I wanted to ask Chad if she'd ever hugged him, but I knew I never would because it would be better not to know.

On Wednesday of that same week, DeAnna invited Chad, Jonathan, and me over for dinner at her house before Mutual.

Both her mom and dad spoke with a slight accent. Her dad had come to the United States without papers. "Without papers" is a polite way of saying he snuck into the country. His first job was running an elevator in a hotel in New York City. At first he didn't speak a word of English, but he smiled at everyone who got on the elevator.

Eventually he learned to say, "Good morning," and "Good afternoon," and "Good evening."

Every day he practiced English on the people who rode on his elevator. Within a few months, he was able to carry on a simple conversation with them.

After a year, his boss came and told him he was the friendliest employee in the hotel and that they weren't going to keep him in the elevator anymore. He was moved instead to the front desk, which was a more prestigious job and paid more. It was a great example of how important it is for immigrants to learn to speak English.

Eventually he somehow learned about the Church, was baptized, met the woman who would be his wife, had her taught by the missionaries and baptized her himself.

He eventually started his own company and used that company to "sponsor" himself, got a tax ID number, applied for citizenship, and after several years became a citizen.

And now he was vice president of an investment firm. He told us, "I have no education. All that I've learned about leadership, I've learned from callings I've had in the Church."

I had never met anyone like him before in my life. I appreciated him taking time to talk to us and teach us.

Chad made the mistake of trying to divert attention from DeAnna's father to himself. He made clever comments, but neither DeAnna's father or mother nor DeAnna herself laughed very much. I'd never seen Chad so off balance, and even though he was my friend, it made me very happy to see it. Mostly because he lost a little ground with DeAnna, and that had to be good for me.

The next night Maria received another discussion from the missionaries. It was the last discussion they usually give before baptism.

At the end of the lesson, Sister Davis told us that she had just been told that she was gong to be transferred on Monday. When Maria heard that, she said she wanted to be baptized before Sister Davis left. Sister Rodriguez asked Maria if she would like to be baptized on Saturday. I didn't understand all of the sentence, but I did recognize the Spanish word for Saturday: sábado.

"Yes," Maria said, in English.

When I got home that night, my mom said I seemed to be spending too much time away from home. Without thinking, I answered, "Sí." And then I told her that Maria and Gabriel were going to be baptized Saturday and that Maria had asked me to baptize her.

I continued. "Gabriel is eight but Kristina is only five. So either Chad or Jonathan can baptize Gabriel. We couldn't decide who, but Sister Rodriguez suggested that one of them give a talk. Jonathan volunteered to do that, so Chad is going to baptize Gabriel."

My mom seemed excited for me and told me what a good preparation this was for my mission.

Her mentioning my mission depressed me. I could hardly wait for the day when I'd have the money I needed to open up my mission account once again.

The baptism service on Saturday was one of the best experiences of my life.

My mom and dad came to the baptism, so they got to meet all my new friends, including DeAnna. Jonathan's mom and dad and Michelle also came. Chad's folks came, too, but they arrived too late for much socializing before the service began.

Two of the women Maria worked with at the meat packing plant also came. Sister Rodriguez and Sister Davis introduced me to them, and Maria proudly told them I was the one who had given her money to help her get papers. They seemed very happy to meet me. I wouldn't have known what was being said except for Sister Rodriguez telling me later.

"Do you ever wonder how many people know you paid for Maria to get a social security card?" DeAnna asked me.

"I didn't before, but I do now. Right now I'm glad my mom and dad don't speak Spanish."

"You haven't told them yet?" she asked.

I sighed. "No, but don't tell Sister Davis, okay?"

She nodded. "I won't, but you really need to let your parents know. It will be better if they hear it from you than from someone else."

"Probably so."

A few minutes later we started the baptism service. There was the usual song and a prayer and then a talk by Sister Rodriguez. She would say a little in Spanish and then say it again in English. She made it seem easy, but I knew it wasn't.

And then Jonathan talked. He did an outstanding job. He gave it both in English and Spanish. He told us his mom had helped him with the Spanish part.

And then it was time for the baptisms. I baptized Maria and then Chad baptized Gabriel.

I was both nervous and excited. Beforehand I worried that I would mess up on the actual language, but that went okay. What was really thrilling was to know that for the first time I was using my priesthood to help someone come into the Church. I'd never done that before, and it was something I knew I would never forget.

In the dressing room as we were changing out of our wet baptismal clothing, Chad and I were as excited as if we'd just won an important football game. At one point my dad stuck his head in the dressing room and asked us to talk quieter because the people waiting could hear us.

After all of us who'd gotten wet returned to the meeting, President Rivera welcomed the newest members of their branch. And then Sister Davis gave a talk on the gift of the Holy Ghost. She said part of it in Spanish. It sounded almost as if Spanish were her natural language. She said how wonderful it had been to be able to help teach Maria and her two kids. And she got emotional as she said it. I hadn't thought of her as someone who ever got real emotional, but she did then.

And then President Rivera announced that Maria wanted to say something. I panicked. I hoped she'd only talk in Spanish so my mom and dad wouldn't find out about the money I'd loaned her. But, no, President Rivera stood next to her and translated into English.

She thanked Chad, Jonathan, and me for bringing her the gospel and being such a big help to her, but thankfully she didn't mention the money. She also thanked Sister Rodriguez and Sister Davis for teaching her and said how grateful she was to the members of the Spanish branch for their love and support. She said she was also very grateful for her new job. Her boss had told her he was going to move her to his office and make her a supervisor because she was learning English so well that she could talk to everyone who worked there. And she thanked DeAnna and Sister Rodriguez and me for teaching her English.

While she was talking, I kept praying that she wouldn't say anything that would tip my mom and dad off about the money I'd loaned her.

My prayers were answered.

After the baptism, the Spanish branch provided food for everyone who attended, even Gringos like my mom and dad.

During the luncheon, Maria kissed my mom on the cheek and told her what a good boy I was. My mom seemed a little surprised by the kiss on the cheek and the hug, but she covered it well. Jonathan's mom, of course, was used to it and hugged back. Chad's folks left before it got to the hugging.

So, all in all, it was a perfect day.

Sunday morning, when I first woke up and thought about what had happened, I felt good about myself and could hardly wait to be called on a mission.

That morning in priesthood meeting, the ward mission leader did what he did every week and that was to encourage us to share the gospel. Usually, I just blew off what he said, but that day I wanted to get up and give a little talk about our accomplishments. I wanted people to know what we'd done for Maria and her family. But I didn't because it would seem too much like bragging.

On Monday at lunch, Jonathan didn't stick around because he had to study for a test. Just after Chad left our table to get some brownies from the table where the anorexic girls ate, DeAnna put her hand on mine briefly. "I want you to know how proud I am of you. I'm grateful I've gotten to know you. You've taught me a lot, Dan. I hope we'll always be friends, even after we graduate and go our separate ways." This was the first time I realized that after we graduated we might not be together anymore. That depressed me.

"What are you going to do after you graduate?" I asked.

"My aunt lives in Tempe, Arizona. That's where Arizona State

University is. She's invited me to go to school there and live with her for free. What about you?"

"I've been accepted to BYU and BYU-Idaho but I'm sure I could be accepted to Arizona State University. I aced the ACT exam."

"Must be nice to be brilliant."

"Yeah, I guess."

"So you might go with me to Tempe for school?"

"Yeah, sure. Why not? That'd be great to be there with you." I paused. "The truth is, my life is a lot better with you in it."

"Mine too, actually."

I thought of telling her that it was a definite possibility that I might be falling in love with her. But I didn't. Because I worried that if I said it, the phrase *definite possibility* would sound too much like a weather report—like "There's a sixty percent possibility of love." Either I was in love with her or I wasn't. And since I didn't know for sure, I figured I'd better just keep my mouth shut. At least for a little while.

We were holding hands until Chad came back and sat down next to DeAnna and draped his arm over her shoulder.

"Chad, I don't think it's a good idea for you to be doing that," I said. "It's actually against the rules here at the school. It's called public display of affection, or PDA for short."

He laughed. "Actually, I'm impressed you've memorized all the rules."

"I'm serious! Get your hands off her!"

Chad moved his arm off her shoulder. "Sorry. I didn't know you had a thing for DeAnna." He shook his head and smiled. "Do you two want me to leave so you two can quote school rules to each other—or whatever you guys do when you're alone together?"

"We don't do anything but talk when we're together. Just like when you and I are together, Chad," DeAnna said.

"Do you want me to leave?" Chad asked DeAnna.

"No," she said. "I want the four of us to always be friends." She sighed. "I want us to be The Four Amigos."

"That's what I want, too," Chad said. "Cowboy, what do you want? To have DeAnna all to yourself?"

"No, I don't want that. I just think it would be better if you weren't draping yourself over her all the time."

"Look, I've got to go. Later, okay?" Chad said.

I thought about telling DeAnna that Chad was right and that I did want her all to myself. But I didn't know how to say it.

"What's happening between us?" she asked.

"I'm not sure, but it does seem to me that things are changing."

"That's the way it seems to me too," she said. "Are you willing to risk your friendship with Chad and Jonathan for us to be closer?"

"I don't know yet."

After my next class I found Chad and told him I was sorry for acting up. He told me it was all right, and that there was bound to be some clashes between us because of DeAnna. "If we can just all stay friends with her, and nothing more, then it'll be okay."

After school, the minute I walked in the house, I could tell that something was wrong. My mom was sitting on the couch with her arms folded. She wasn't one to sit around like that, and she looked as though she was very disturbed.

"Hi, Mom," I said.

"Please sit down," she said sternly.

I sat down.

I figured somebody in my family had died.

"Today in the mail," my mom said, "we received bank statements for all our savings accounts. Except they didn't send a statement for your mission savings account."

Suddenly I felt like I couldn't breathe. "Well, they probably just forgot."

"I thought that might be the case. So I went down personally and inquired. Imagine my surprise when I found out you recently took out all the money and closed the account. I would like to know why you did that."

"Good question." I needed time to come up with a good excuse. "Can I get something to drink first?"

"No, you may not. There was, according to their records, nearly seven hundred and fifty dollars in that account at the beginning of December. And now there's nothing. In fact, there's not even an account. What did you do with the money?"

I heard the garage door open, and a short time later it closed. That meant my dad was home early. That wasn't good. He walked into the room, glared at me, and said to my mom, "Has he told you yet what he did with the money?"

"No, not yet."

He stood over me. "We need answers, and we need them now. Are you on drugs?"

I laughed. Maybe too much.

"Your mother and I don't consider this a laughing matter, young man," my dad said. "What did you do with nearly eight hundred dollars?"

I sighed.

"Do you have a gambling problem?" my dad asked.

"No."

"Did you spend it on internet pornography?" he asked.

"No."

"Did you secretly buy a car we don't know about?"

"No."

My mom didn't appreciate this line of questioning. "I don't think you need to put ideas into his mind. Just let him answer the question of what he did with the money."

"I asked you a simple question. Why is this taking so long to get an answer from you?" my dad raged at me. And then I understood. Part of the reason he was so angry was that he'd been called home from work because of me. He had much more important things to do before six-thirty, when he usually got home.

I decided there was a good chance he might go back to work if I answered all his questions. So I simply said, "I loaned it to Maria."

"Is Maria some girl at school?"

"No. She's the woman I baptized Saturday," I said.

"Why did you loan her money?"

"She needed money for rent and for food." That was as far as I was prepared to go.

"How much was her rent?"

"Four hundred dollars. I put in two hundred dollars. Chad and Jonathan put in a hundred each."

"Do their parents know about this?" my mom asked.

"Jonathan's parents know, but not Chad's."

My dad continued. "That only comes to two hundred dollars from your account. Where did the rest of the money go?"

I sighed. This was not going to be good. But I had to tell them if I wanted my dad to leave and go back to work and quit harassing me.

I took a deep breath. "Actually, I loaned Maria five hundred dollars to get a fake social security card. She can't get a real one, you know, because she's not a citizen. But I guess there's places in town where you can buy fake ones."

My mom gasped. My dad banged his fist on the wall and began pacing. "Do you realize Maria and you have broken the law and that you both could go to federal prison?"

I shrugged. "Only if she's caught. And that probably won't happen."

"What makes you so sure it won't happen?" my dad asked.

"If it was going to happen, it would have already happened to the ten million illegal aliens already in the country. I'd say statistics are on my side, wouldn't you?"

That set him off. "You know what? I'm calling the Federal

authorities now and reporting what you did! Now that your mother and I know about this, we become accessories to the crime unless we report it. I'm calling them now!" He went to the phone.

My mom stood up. "You are not reporting our son! All he was trying to do was to help!"

"It doesn't matter what he was trying to do!" my dad argued. "The fact remains, he's broken the law."

I started for the kitchen. "You two work this out. I'm going to get something to eat."

That really set my Dad off. "Go to your room!" he shouted.

"Yeah, sure, no problemo, as they say in Espanol."

On my way to my room, I stopped in the kitchen long enough to grab some bananas on the counter so I'd have something to eat.

In my room, I finished a banana and turned on my TV.

I need to tell you more about my family so you'll understand what my dad did next. My next older brother is Kevin. He's eight years older than me. When he was in ninth grade, he got into drugs big time. Over the next year my parents tried everything they could think of to get him away from his friends who were using, but nothing seemed to work. They pleaded with him to stop. They had the bishop meet with him. They got him into a group therapy with others his age. But none of that worked.

Finally my dad got hold of a book that talked about tough love. He decided to try it out. So one night when Kevin got home, he found that his room was completely empty. No bed, no dresser, no clothes, no laptop, no TV. Nothing but a blanket and a pillow. My dad had also put his long board, his mountain bike, his snow board into storage.

My dad told Kevin he could earn back those privileges, one at a time, by obeying some rules he and my mom had set up for him. If he refused to do that, we were all piling into the car and driving him to a three month wilderness camp for troubled youth run by ex-Marine sergeants.

Kevin bought into the program. Gradually, he got a new set of friends and turned his life around. Now he had a college degree, was married with two kids, and had a good job in Detroit. So, since tough love had been so successful with Kevin, my dad was about to try it on me.

A minute later I heard my dad coming up the stairs, and I lobbed the rest of the bananas into my closet.

He burst into my room, unplugged my TV, and hauled it out of the room. And then he came back for my CD player.

Over the next few minutes I watched as he hauled my mattress and box springs out of the room, leaving me only a few blankets and a pillow. He propped the mattress and box springs against the wall in the hallway.

Finally he came and took my PC and printer. "You can earn these back by following the new rules we're going to implement around here."

"Yeah sure, Dad, whatever you say," I said, trying to sound like I wasn't the rebel he thought I was.

And then he left again.

I could hear my mother coming up the stairs. She must have seen everything he'd taken from my room. "You're taking his bed away?"

"Yes, I am! The reason he's got into this trouble in the first place is that he has way too many privileges."

"Since when is a bed a privilege!" she shot back.

"He can earn back his bed if he follows our new rules for him."

Next my dad used a hammer and screwdriver to remove the door to my room.

"What on earth are you doing now?" my mom asked. "You think a door is a privilege, too?"

"That's right. I do."

"I suppose he can earn that back, too?" she asked sarcastically.

"In time, I'm sure he can."

"And what is the purpose of all this?"

"He needs to understand that if he serves time in a federal prison, he's not going to have any privacy at all." He set the door out in the hall with everything else.

"Michael, this is ridiculous. Daniel is not Kevin. You and I need to talk about this downstairs now."

I was loving this. Well, not really. It actually saddened me. I was the good son, not the rebellious one. When Kevin was giving them so much grief, I did my best to do everything right so they wouldn't have to worry about me too. The only trouble with that is that sometimes I felt like they took me for granted.

I finished off the other bananas and then started working on my homework. About half an hour later my mom came to the open space where a door used to be. "Your father and I need to talk to you downstairs."

"I'm not done with my homework."

"Daniel Winchester, do not make this any harder than it needs to be!" The way she said it was as though she were pleading with me. I decided I'd better do what she said, so I followed her down the stairs.

I sat on an old overstuffed chair which I had been told was my grandfather's favorite. My mom and dad sat on the couch facing me. My dad had a spiral notebook on his lap.

"Your mother and I have come up with a three-point program for you," my dad said. He looked down at his notes. "Our first requirement is that you pay back the money you stole from your mission account."

"I think the word stole is a little harsh," my mom said softly.

He scowled, then reworded it, "The money you withdrew from your mission account without our permission." He sighed. "All of which came from your grandfather, who on his death bed requested that money be given to you for your mission."

"I plan on putting the money back as soon as Maria pays me back," I said.

That set my dad off again. "You think you're ever going to see a penny of that money back from her? It's not going to happen. Those people take and take and take, but they never give back."

"That's not true. She's already returned five dollars to me. It's in my closet. Let's see. Five dollars is five hundred pennies, right?"

My dad glared at my mom like this was all her fault to have a mouthy son like me.

My dad continued. "Second. You will get a job and work after school and all day Saturdays. I just talked to a friend of mine who runs a plumbing supply wholesale store just out of town. Last week he told me that he needs someone to help out. He's willing to see how you work out. I'll pick you up at school tomorrow and run you out there."

"What if Maria pays back all the money, say, next week?" I asked.

"You'll still work there. You need to earn money for your mission. Apparently you have too much time on your hands. This will cure that. And don't think of sloughing off on your school work, either. When I was your age, I held down a part-time job and still managed to get good grades. I will expect the same kind of performance from you."

It was hard to take this without standing up for myself in some way, so I stuck my index finger in my ear to see if I could get any ear wax from it. This was, I guess, my version of wild teenage rebellion. Some people get drunk, I go on an expedition for ear wax.

"Are you even listening to your father?" my mom asked.

"Yeah, why do you ask?"

"Get your finger out of your ear then."

I looked at my finger. I hadn't gotten any ear wax out, but there was no way they could know that, so I wiped my finger on the sweatshirt they'd given me for Christmas.

My dad was ready to proceed. "Third, you will quit attending church in the Spanish branch. It is clear to me that they have been a bad influence on you."

"I will not quit going to the Spanish branch! In the first place, I attend our ward first. Certainly you can't forbid me from going to even more church meetings. That wouldn't make any sense."

"You will do what I say, young man!"

"Or you'll what?" I challenged him. "Kick me out of the house?"

"If that's what it takes!"

"I don't want my son living with some other family!" my mom said.

"Then he needs to act like our son."

"Why is it so bad if he goes to two sacrament meetings a week, two Sunday Schools, and two priesthood meetings?" she complained "I don't think many in our ward would be sympathetic if we told them our son is too religious."

My dad was so mad at my mom he couldn't control himself. "I'm going to the garage," my dad said. "There's something out there I need to fix."

I watched him hurry out to the garage. I remember thinking, That's what I would have done.

"Dan, will you do me a favor while your father is in the garage?" my mom asked. Her voice was subdued now.

"What?"

"Move your bed back into your room, bring the banana peels from upstairs and put them in the garbage, and make your bed."

"What about my PC? I use it to do my homework."

She sighed. "All, right. You can put that back, too."

"Thanks, Mom."

As I was on my way up the stairs, she called after me.

I stopped on the stairs. "Yeah, Mom?"

"I know you only meant well . . . I mean with the money."

That got to me big time. She understood what I was trying to do, and she still loved me. She deserved for me to have a better attitude. "I did, Mom. I meant well. I really did."

"I know. I love you, Dan."

I was finding it hard now to be my family's hardened criminal. "I love you too, Mom. Thanks . . . for everything."

With that I continued up the stairs.

As I moved the bed back into my room, one thing was certain. Because of my mom, I would continue to live at home.

I have to admit, though, that in some ways I was a little disappointed.

Chapter Eight

Ibegan working at a plumbing supply store after school and on Saturdays. Most of our business came from plumbing contractors who knew where everything was, so I didn't have to find it for them. Whatever they bought they had me put it on their account. They weren't much for talking. They came to the counter, plunked down what they were getting, then said something like, "Well, that ought to do it for today."

I didn't have much to do, so when I had time I'd sweep the floor or wash the windows. Later, my boss had me help him with billing.

The store was about two miles from where we lived. At first my mom took me to work and picked me up. After about a week though, she talked to my dad about them buying me a car so I could drive myself. I told them I'd pay them back.

My dad was against the idea at first, saying he didn't like rewarding me for having taken money from my mission account without their permission. But my mom's argument won the day. "Then you start taking him out there and back every day!"

The next Saturday my dad and I went car shopping. We ended up getting a junker for nine hundred dollars. And then we went home and worked out the rules for my use of the car. My dad emphasized that the car was only to be used to get me to and from work, and that I was not to use it for any other purpose.

With me working I didn't see DeAnna as much, which was my loss and Chad's gain. He was with her almost every day after school. Jonathan spent time with her, too, but not as much.

Sometimes, though, DeAnna would call me at work just to talk. Since I was alone in the store a lot, I liked the diversion.

Once, though, the boss came in the back door, I guess to check up on me.

He must have listened to my part of the conversation—enough to know it wasn't a customer.

"Who are you talking to?" he asked.

"My girlfriend," I said, wondering if DeAnna could hear that.

"I don't mind you talking when all your work is done and there's no customers, but not on this phone. Get yourself a cell phone."

So I did. I put enough money down for them to start giving me service. Which meant more payments.

My boss limited me to ten minutes a day talking to DeAnna. He gave me a timer so when he came in, if I was on the phone with her, he'd know how long I'd been talking. I told him I'd honor his request, and mostly I did.

DeAnna kept saying she wished we could spend more time together, even though I knew Chad was keeping her busy on weekends especially.

One Sunday morning just before priesthood in our ward, Chad told me he'd kissed DeAnna the night before on a date.

"You kissed her?" I asked.

"Yep, twice actually."

"How was it?"

"Totally amazing!"

"Great," I said, trying to disguise how jealous I was.

"She's falling for me big time," he said.

"Why?"

"My best guess is my stunning manly looks and great personality."

The depressing thing was I agreed with him. "Great," I muttered. "Let's go to priesthood."

"Wait. Don't you want to know all the details?" Chad asked. Even with his fun personality, he could really be irritating.

"No."

After that I assumed that DeAnna was exclusively Chad's. The really strange thing was that she still kept phoning me at work. I couldn't figure out why, but I didn't ask her because I enjoyed talking to her.

With my working so much, I didn't get to spend as much time with Maria and her kids during the week, but I always saw them on Sunday afternoons when I attended the Spanish branch. Every two weeks when Maria was paid, she gave Chad, Jonathan and me ten dollars each to help pay back what we'd given her.

Maria was continuing to learn how to speak English from Sister Rodriguez and had learned enough to carry on a simple conversation. Her husband Eduardo was still in Mexico, but she still expected him any day. Because of her English skills her boss put her in the office and gave her a raise.

I didn't see Jonathan much either. When I did go over to see him, it was obvious that his sister Michelle had forgotten I used to be her hero. She didn't seem to have any interest in me anymore. Is that any way to treat a hero?

So that was my life. I worked six days a week. I went to school. I did my homework. And on Sundays I went to church for six hours.

One good thing, though, was that I had a car and a cell phone. I also liked having a little money that I could call my own, although most of every paycheck had to go toward paying for my car, my cell phone, and repaying the money that had been in my mission savings account. In order for me to pay my bills more easily, I opened a checking account.

One thing that the Four Amigos did in school that was fun was to sing in a school talent show. It was, of course, Chad's idea. In fact he signed us up without even talking to us. On the night of the talent show, we came out wearing big sombreros we'd borrowed from the drama department. We sang the song *The Ballad of the Three Amigos* except we changed the lyrics to four amigos. Because we got a standing ovation, Chad, Jonathan and I sang *My Little Buttercup*, to DeAnna.

One Friday in mid-March, Maria and DeAnna came to the store just before closing. They looked really stressed. DeAnna said, "We need your help."

"What do you need?"

"Eduardo hurt, very bad," Maria said. I could tell she'd been crying.

DeAnna explained. "He made it across the border without any trouble. He was traveling by bus. When he got to Las Vegas, he had to change to a bus going to Salt Lake City. He had a couple of hours to wait, so he decided to take a walk. That's when he got beat up and robbed. He called Maria and talked to her. I guess he's pretty badly hurt. And he's out of money and they took the bus ticket too."

That was horrible news, but I still couldn't see why they were coming to me.

"We need to drive down there and pick him up," DeAnna explained. "You have a car. Can you drive us to Las Vegas and back?"

That was a complication I didn't need, and I knew my parents wouldn't be happy about it. Even so, I sighed and said quietly, "Yeah, sure, I guess so."

"I'll go with you to translate," DeAnna said.

"The only problem is I'm not sure what to tell my folks," I said.

"Maybe you could tell them you're going to stay at Chad's tonight."

"Good idea."

"I'll call and ask him if he'll cover for you," she said.

"One thing, though," I said. "I don't want Chad to go with us."

"I don't, either." She started to blush. "What I mean is that with Maria, Gabriel, Kristina, you and me, and with Eduardo coming back with us, there won't be room."

I called my mom and told her about Chad wanting me to stay at his house, and said that I would be going there right after work. She was hesitant but finally said that was okay. But she wanted me to stop by and pick up my pajamas and my toothbrush. I told her I'd borrow something from Chad. Her last bit of advice was to make sure I flossed before bed. That made me feel even more guilty. Here I was about to drive to Nevada and back in one night in a car that wasn't all that safe, and my mom was worrying about my teeth.

A few minutes later we were on our way. DeAnna sat in the front seat with me while Maria, Gabriel, and Kristina sat in the backseat.

When we had been on the road about half an hour, Eduardo called. Maria spoke to him in Spanish for a minute or two and then said something in Spanish to DeAnna, explaining what was happening, "The men who beat him up are circling the block in their car. He's afraid they might come back and kill him."

"I can't get there any faster," I said.

"He says there's a motel across the street from where he is. If he goes there, can he have the manager call you, so you can arrange for him to get a room." She paused. "It will mean you'll have to pay the manager when we arrive. Can you do that?"

I shrugged. "I guess so. I have my check book with me."

"Okay, good." DeAnna turned to tell Maria what I'd said, and then Maria told Eduardo.

A few minutes later Maria got another call. She gave it to DeAnna. "That's right," she said.

A minute later she handed me Maria's cell phone. "It's the manager of the motel. He wants to talk to you about getting paid for the room."

"Hello?" I said.

"I got one question for you. How can you guarantee I'm not going to get taken if I give José here a room?" He said José like it was a swear word.

"We're coming down to get him. I'll pay you for the room when we get there."

"And when will that be?"

I wasn't actually sure how long it would take to get to Las Vegas, so I could only guess. "Four or five hours I think."

"And how are you going to pay me?"

"With a check."

"We don't take out-of-town checks."

"This is an emergency. Can't you make an exception?"

"Why should I? Let me tell you something. This guy is a mess. There's blood all over him. I'm going to have to charge you a cleanup fee. And what's this all about anyway? Is José here in some kind of a drug ring? Because that's mostly what we get from these people."

"His name isn't José. It's Eduardo. He was waiting for a bus. He decided to take a walk. He was attacked and beat up. We'd like to let him have a place where he can be safe until we get there."

"Why are you involved in this?"

"I like to help out people when they're going through a hard time."

"Why?"

I paused, trying to think of a reason that would make sense to him. "Maybe because I'm an Eagle Scout."

He swore, but in a way that showed respect. "You're an Eagle Scout?"

"Yes."

"I have a grandson who's an Eagle Scout."

"That's great. It's not easy to get."

"He's the kind of a boy who'd do something stupid like help José here out when he's in a tight spot."

"As Scouts we're taught to help people whenever we can."

"Okay, I'll tell you what I'll do. I'll give him the room, but you be sure and stop by and pay for the room when you get here."

"I will. Thank you very much. See you soon." I ended the call then turned toward DeAnna. "Tell Maria that the manager is going to give Eduardo a room. I'll pay for it when we get there."

When Maria got the news, she leaned forward, and patted me on the back and said over and over, "Gracias." She knew I could understand that.

Within an hour Maria and her kids were taking a nap.

"Can I tell you something?" DeAnna said.

"I guess so."

"You're a lot like the Good Samaritan."

"No, I'm not. Not really."

"You are to me."

"Thanks."

"I respect you, and I trust you."

"That's great," I said. I meant it to be pleasant but it came out sounding a little bitter.

"Are you mad at me?"

Actually, I was. "You respect me, but Chad is the one you end up kissing."

"Did he tell you that?"

"Yes."

"I should have known he'd brag to you about it. This won't make sense to you, but the truth is I didn't kiss him. He kissed me. And it was just that one time."

"He said he kissed you twice."

"But it was one quick kiss and then another one. It happened before I had time to react to it. That's just like him, isn't it? To brag to you about his victories."

"Let's not talk about it anymore, okay?" I said.

"Chad asks me out, but you never do. Why's that?"

"Chad is my friend."

"So you not asking me out is because you're being loyal to Chad. Why don't you be loyal to me? Why does he take preference as a friend over me?"

It felt good to know that she wanted to go out with me. "I've known him a lot longer."

She shook her head. "You're right. We shouldn't talk about this. I just find it sad that I can't be with a guy I care about more than anyone else."

"If you care so much about me, why did you make out with Chad?"

"I didn't make out with him!"

"Look, I don't blame you. With anything involving Chad and me, I always come in a distant second."

"Not to me you don't."

We drove for several minutes without talking, and then she said, "There's something I haven't told you."

"What?"

"I went to Chad first and asked him to drive us to Las Vegas. He turned me down."

"Why?"

"He told me his folks would never let him."

"Mine wouldn't, either, if they knew."

"That was just an excuse. I think it was just because he didn't want to go to that much trouble to help someone out. He's not like you."

I shook my head. "I would never turn you down."

"If that's true, then I'm asking you to start seeing me more often."

I nodded but didn't say anything.

"What do you want me to do, get on my knees and beg you?" she asked.

"If we start seeing each other exclusively, it will be the end of the Four Amigos."

"Look, just forget about it, okay? I will never bring this up again."

We didn't say much for a long time.

I couldn't figure this out. Chad had always been the one I looked up to and wanted to be like. So why didn't DeAnna feel that way about him? It didn't make sense.

It actually took us six hours to get to Las Vegas. By the time we got there, it was a little after midnight. Once we were in town, I had DeAnna call the manager and have him give us directions.

It didn't look like a motel I would ever stay in. It was old and shabby, with the T not working in the neon Motel sign. After we pulled up to the office, I went in to pay for the room.

I explained who I was.

"How old are you?" the clerk asked.

"Old enough to have a checking account and a car," I said.

"Who's in the car with you?"

"Eduardo's wife and his two kids. And I brought along a translator so I can know what's going on."

"And that's all?"

"Yes, why?"

"I just don't want to end up with thirty people in the same room like has happened before with you people."

"My people? My people are from Sweden and Scotland. You get a lot of them here?"

"You know what I mean. Okay, the room will be ninety-seven dollars. I already added in cleanup costs."

The balance in my checking account was 24 dollars, but I wrote the check anyway, signed it, and handed it to him.

He studied the check. "Is this your current address and phone number?"

"Yes, it is."

"You sure about that?"

"Yes, I am."

"Okay." He took the check, put it in the till, and gave me a key and directions to the room.

All of us would have to walk past him to get to our room.

I returned to the car. "It's all taken care of."

The two kids were still asleep. "I'll get Gabriel. DeAnna, can you get Kristina?" I asked.

"Okay."

As we walked past the manager on our way to the room, I noticed the way he leered at DeAnna. The look on his face was a mixture of disgust and lust.

"So, is Chiquita here your so-called translator?" he asked cynically when it was just us in the lobby.

"Yes."

"Yeah, sure, and pigs can fly. You sure you're an Eagle Scout?"

"I am. She's my friend. That's all. She's actually seeing another guy."

"Your loss then."

"Yeah, big time."

As I turned to leave him, he called out, "Don't forget to move your car. Where you're at now is just for people who are checking in."

"Okay."

I used the key to open the door and then let Maria be the first one into the room. DeAnna held the door for me so I could get in with Gabriel in my arms. She came in after me, carrying Kristina.

Maria ran to Eduardo who was lying on one of the beds. There was blood on the pillowcase under his head.

Eduardo sat up when we came in. His face was swollen, and there was blood on his face and T-shirt.

When Maria saw him, she began to cry and then took his battered face into her hands, kissing him on his forehead and murmuring something I couldn't understand. Then she went into the bathroom and came back with a damp washcloth and a towel. She had him lay down while she attended to him, carefully wiping the blood off his face.

Kristina, now awake and seeing her daddy in such bad shape, started crying. DeAnna picked her up and, in Spanish, told her that her daddy had been hurt, but that he was going to be all right, and just needed to rest up. Gabriel was also awake now, and I held him in my arms, and we stood next to the bed where he could watch his mom making things better.

After Maria got Eduardo cleaned up, she sat with him on the bed and held his hand while he rested. She said something to DeAnna. She nodded and then translated it for me.

"She wonders if we can stay here overnight, before we drive back. She doesn't want him to travel until he feels a little better."

I panicked. I needed to be at work in the morning, and if I wasn't, my mom and dad would find out.

While I was worrying about that, the phone in the room rang. I figured it was just the manager reminding me to move my car. "Yeah?" I said.

It was my dad. "Is it true you're in some motel in Las Vegas, Nevada with a bunch of Mexicans?"

I sat down on the second bed and struggled to catch my breath.

"The reason I know about this is that the manager just called me and told me you just wrote a check for ninety seven dollars. He wanted to know if you had that much money in your account? What should I have told him?"

I set the phone on the bed and covered my face with my hands.

"What's wrong?" DeAnna asked.

I gave a big sigh. "It's my dad."

"How does he know we're here?"

"The manager called to make sure the check I gave him was okay. Our home phone number was on the check."

We could hear my dad demanding I talk to him.

"You'd better talk to him," DeAnna said.

I closed my eyes. "He's going to kill me."

"Just tell him why you're here. He'll understand."

I picked up the phone again. "Dad, are you still there? Yes, we're in Las Vegas. But I can explain."

"What did I tell you about using that car?" he yelled.

"It's just for going to and from work."

"Did I say it would be all right to drive without permission to Las Vegas in the middle of the night?"

"No. I can explain though."

"The manager says you also got some hot Senorita your age in there with you. What in blazes is going on?"

"Dad, can I talk to Mom please?"

"He wants to talk to you!" my dad said angrily to my mom.

"Dan, is that you?" my mom asked.

"Hi, Mom," I said.

"I know there must be a good reason why you drove to Las Vegas tonight, and why you're with the people you're with. Please tell me."

"You remember Maria, the woman I baptized? Well, I'm here with her and her two kids, Gabriel and Kristina, and also with Maria's husband, Eduardo. DeAnna came with us to translate for me. Eduardo made it across the border okay but he got beat up pretty bad and robbed once he got to Las Vegas. He called Maria to come and get him but she doesn't have a car, so she asked me and that's why we're here."

"What's he doing in a motel with those people?" my dad asked loudly . . .

"Your father wants to know. . . "

"I heard him. On the way here Eduardo called and told Maria that the men who beat him up were circling the block. He was afraid they wanted to kill him. So he asked if I'd pay for him to be in a motel room until we arrived. I told him I'd do that."

"Let me talk to him," my dad said. To me he asked, "You wrote a check for the motel room?"

"Yes."

"Do you have enough money in your checking account to cover the amount?"

"Not right now. I thought I'd put money in the account when I got home."

"Where will you get the money to do that?" my dad asked.

I sighed. "Can I borrow some from you? I'll pay you back."

My dad pretty much lost it after that. He started going on about me having some big fiesta in our motel room with the Mexicans and some "low-life" girl that he accused me of picking up off the streets in Las Vegas.

My mom came to my rescue. "The girl with him is DeAnna. We met her at Maria's baptism. She eats lunch with Chad, Jonathan and Dan at school. She's a member of the Church."

Even that didn't help ease my dad's anger. He went several minutes complaining about me writing a check with no funds in my account to cover it. He told me I could go to jail for that. Finally, he said, "Stay there, I'm coming to get you."

"Dad, I appreciate you being so willing to help us get Maria, Eduardo, Gabriel and Kristina back to their apartment, and to get DeAnna home, but really, I can do this by myself, without your help."

"You think I care about those others? They can all walk back to Mexico for all I care!"

DeAnna must have heard my dad's ranting. She went to Maria and started talking to her quietly in Spanish. Maria then leaned down and asked Eduardo something. He sat up and then stood up. They got up and left the room. DeAnna waited behind for me.

"Just a minute, Dad," I said. "What's up?" I asked DeAnna.

"Eduardo says he feels good enough to travel. They've gone to the car. Let's head back."

"Dad, sorry to interrupt, but we're heading back home now. See you in the morning. I'll be all right. You get some sleep, okay?"

"You stay there! I'm coming to get you!"

"We're leaving now, Dad. Don't worry. If I get tired, I'll have DeAnna drive. I think Maria can drive, too, and maybe even Eduardo. So we'll be okay. Don't worry about us."

"Do any of these Mexicans have drivers' licenses?"

"DeAnna does for sure. I'll have her drive when I get tired. Bye, Dad. I love you."

I ended the call and followed the others out to the car. Before we even got to the car, my cell phone rang. I knew it was my dad so I turned it off.

We started back again. It was one o'clock in the morning.

Gabriel and Kristina were asleep before we got to the Interstate, and after talking quietly to each other for a little while, Maria and Eduardo both fell asleep too.

"Are you going to be able to stay awake?" DeAnna asked.

"Yeah, sure, no problemo." I turned to her and smiled. "You must be so impressed I'm learning Spanish so quickly, right?"

"Yeah, something like that. What do you think your dad will do?"

"Well, let's see. By the time I get home, he'll have taken the door off my room so I won't have any privacy, and he'll have hauled my bed to the garage so I'll have to sleep on the floor. Oh, and he'll tell me what a disappointment I am to him and my mom. Oh, and also, he'll sell my car and take my cell phone away. Other than that, not much."

"I'm sorry."

I looked into my rearview mirror at Maria, Eduardo, Kristina and Gabriel sleeping in the backseat. They were together again. "I'm not. I don't regret what I did."

"What you did was very noble. I will always remember it."

"You know when you were talking about the Good Samaritan? Right now I'm thinking maybe there's a part to that story we've never heard. Like when the Good Samaritan got home, maybe his wife told him he was a fool to waste money on a stranger and that he was never going to get the money back."

"And if he did have a wife like that, so what?" she asked. "Does it really matter? What matters is that he cared about someone in trouble. Like you did tonight. Are you going to be all right, I mean with your mom and dad? Because if you want, I can go in with you to talk to them."

"No, I'll be okay. I already know what they're going to say. How disappointed they are in me. I guess I'd better get used to that. I'll be disappointing them until I leave for my mission. And then they'll give a sigh of relief and tell each other they're glad that's over. And when I get back from my mission, I'll spend a week at home and then leave and never return again, except for a short visit once in a while. Because I don't need their version of what's right and what's wrong. How can they say it was wrong of me to help Maria and her kids? That's what I don't understand. I will never understand that."

"They're good people though," she said.

"Look, I really don't want to talk about this."

It was quiet for a while, and then she started singing to me in Spanish. I didn't understand much of what the songs were about, but it helped calm me down.

After about two hours I was too wiped out to stay awake so I asked her to drive.

I slept for about an hour but then woke up and felt better. My job now was to keep her awake.

By then I must have been really tired because I heard myself saying to her, "You are the most beautiful girl I've ever known. Every time I see you, it like takes my breath away. For me it's like the first time I saw the Grand Canyon."

She laughed. "So, what are you saying? I'm a good example of water erosion?"

"Also, I love the color of your skin. It's like polished wood, walnut I think."

"Anything else in nature you want to compare me with? Earth-quakes, tornadoes?"

"Oh, and I love your hair. My fantasy is to have your hair completely covering my face."

She smiled. "They'd never put that on a greeting card, so it must be coming from you."

"It is. I think I love you. In fact, I'm sure I love you."

"That's just a lack of sleep talking now. I'll disregard all of it, okay?"

"How do you feel about me?" I asked.

"You're the best friend I've ever had. Sometimes I think I love you, like now for instance. But at other times you're just a friend."

"I understand."

"Are you prepared to break up the Four Amigos just so we can be, well, just the two of us in love?" she asked.

I sighed. "I'm not sure."

"Weird, isn't it?" she asked. "That we aren't sure what we want to do even though we love each other."

"Yeah, it is." I paused. "Oh, something you should know. I applied to Arizona State University last week."

"You did? How come you're just now telling me?"

"I was going to wait until I'm accepted. Also, I'll probably need a scholarship to be able to afford going there. It's a lot more expensive than BYU-Idaho."

"So we might end up being at Arizona State together our freshman year?" she asked.

"Yeah. Until I leave on my mission."

"Where do you want to go on your mission?" she asked.

"Anywhere where I have to learn a language and that isn't in the United States. Actually, I think I'd like to go to Ecuador and meet all your family."

"That'd be good, especially if we . . . uh . . . get together after your mission."

"Yeah, that's what I was thinking."

"But you'll go wherever you're called, right?"

"Yeah, I will."

"You'll be an awesome missionary."

"It's what I've always wanted. Sometimes I can hardly wait, and then, at other times, especially when I think about leaving you, I kind of dread going."

"It will be for the best for both of us if you serve a mission."

"I know."

She leaned over and kissed me on the cheek. "We're getting a little ahead of ourselves, aren't we?"

"Yeah, probably so."

She got sleepy after a while so I had her pull over. We fell asleep in each other's arms for a couple of hours and then I drove the rest of the way.

By the time we got to town, it was nearly nine in the morning. I dropped Maria and her family off first and then drove to DeAnna's home.

"My mom and dad will want to know everything that happened, but that's okay. We have nothing to hide. We did the right thing." She kissed me on the cheek. "Good luck with your folks."

"Thanks. You, too."

She hurried inside.

A few minutes later, when I pulled into our driveway, my dad came out. "Get inside right now!" he snapped.

"Actually, that's what I was going to do."

Once we were in the house, he turned on me. My mom, although silent, joined him in his tirade.

He began wagging his finger at me. "Well, let me tell you something! You've really done it this time! That car is gone! I'm getting rid of it tomorrow. And, another thing, give me your cell phone!"

I handed him my cell phone. He told me it was gone too.

So far this was going just the way I thought it would go. They asked a bunch of questions that he didn't expect me to answer. Like "What if you'd been in an accident and gotten yourself killed and everyone else in the car?"

I suspected (correctly) that my dad had already taken off the door to my room and most likely had hauled my bed to the garage, but, even so, I was still hoping to retain a few blankets and maybe even a pillow. So I kept my smart-off answers to myself.

My mom asked me what people might think if they found out I'd gone to Las Vegas with DeAnna and that we'd ended up in a motel together.

"If they know we were with Maria and Eduardo and their kids, and that we were in the motel like maybe thirty minutes max, I don't think they'd be too worried."

"What about the money you've wasted on this trip?" my dad asked.

"Maria and Eduardo will pay me back."

"Did they say they'd pay you back?" my dad asked.

"Not exactly, but I'm sure they will."

"No, they won't! They'll skip town some night, and you'll never hear from them again."

"That's not true."

"You don't know these people like I do. Now go to your room."

"Are you hungry?" my mom asked.

My dad intervened. "I don't care if he's hungry or not! It's time for him to go to work."

My mom got mad and told my dad that I needed to get a little sleep before I went to work. She called my boss and said I'd be coming in at noon.

I went to my room to get some sleep. My bed was gone. Good thing

I had my air mattress. I blew it up, folded my blanket in two and crawled in.

I was a little worried that I wouldn't be able to get to sleep because of all the conflict. I wondered if I should feel guilty but decided that the only thing I had done wrong was not to ask for permission.

And I took comfort in the idea that maybe the Good Samaritan also got chewed out by his wife when he arrived home and told her how much money he'd paid to the innkeeper for the man who'd been robbed and beaten.

And so with that thought in my mind, I quickly fell asleep.

Two hours later my dad woke me up and drove me to work. Because of everything that had already been said, we didn't say a word to each other in the car on our way to the store.

Chapter Nine

After that, my life was one dreary task piled on top of another. I went to school and then to work and then went home and did homework. On Saturdays I worked all day. On Sundays I went to my home ward and then hung out in my room the rest of the day since my folks wouldn't let me attend the Spanish branch anymore. Their excuse was that the branch was just for those who were Hispanic. So I usually didn't get to see DeAnna on Sundays.

Twice a month, at church, Maria would hand DeAnna ten dollars and ask her to give it to me the next time she saw me. It was to pay me back for helping her with rent and a social security card. At first, when I received the money, I'd tell my dad about it, so he'd know that Maria was paying me back. But he was never impressed. He said she'd never completely pay off the loan. And when I insisted she would, he'd bring up how much money in interest I would have earned if I'd never given her the money and ask if she was going to pay that back, too.

My dad still worried about the consequences of me paying for Maria's fake social security card. And anytime he read about a raid by ICE on some company where they found undocumented workers, some with fake social security cards, he made sure I knew about it.

We met once with Mr. Farrentino, a lawyer he had recommended to him. My dad wanted us to contact ICE and admit what I'd done, but Mr. Farrentino suggested we wait. "Maybe nothing will come of this," he said.

We worked out a plan. If I was pulled in for questioning by ICE, I would immediately call my dad, and he'd contact Mr. Farrentino. "Don't talk to them without me there with you," Mr. Farrentino warned me.

"What if I'm not near a phone?" I asked.

"Do you have a cell phone?" Mr. Farrentino asked.

My dad gave me back my cell phone the same day. At the same time he told me how much our visit with Mr. Farrentino had cost him. I'm sure he did it to make me feel guilty, but what it did was make me want to become a lawyer.

By April Conference weekend, by my so-called "good behavior," I earned my bedroom door back and a week after that my bed. I never got the TV that used to be in my room though.

I'm sure my dad thought he was teaching me a lesson when he emptied my bedroom. But the truth was I never regretted driving Maria and her kids to rescue Eduardo. They needed my help, and I would have done it again if they had asked me to do so.

For the rest of April, on those long, lonely Sunday afternoons in my room, when I was missing not being with my friends in the Hispanic Branch, I'd think again about the parable of the Good Samaritan. How the Good Samaritan didn't agonize about what people would think about him helping, or wonder if he could really afford to help out, or worry about how much time he'd lose if he stopped to help. I decided the way the Jews thought about the Samaritans is a lot like some people think about undocumented workers from Central and South America. Distrusted by some, despised by others, invisible to most.

At first I justified what I'd done by the parable of the Good Samaritan, but after a while, I began to see where I'd gone wrong. It wasn't that I drove to Las Vegas to help Maria and Eduardo that was wrong. What was wrong was that I'd tried to cover it up. I'd have been a lot better off if, once we were on the road, I'd called my dad and told him what we were doing. He would have told me no, and I would have respectfully told them I was going anyway and that I'd call him when we got there and for him not to worry.

That's what I should have done. It's never a good idea to cover up the truth.

Once in a while DeAnna would visit me at work. If I had a customer, she'd wait until he left and then we'd talk. She'd always tell me about Maria and her family and how well they were doing.

Sometimes I wanted to tell her again that I thought she was the most beautiful girl in the world but, of course, I never did because we were the Four Amigos, and I didn't want to ruin that. At least not until after graduation.

When it was just the two of us together, she always called me Dan, but, when the four of us were together at lunch, she called me Cowboy.

Once she brought a soccer ball to my work. I stood just outside the store with the door open so I'd be able to hear the phone. And I watched as she dribbled the ball with her feet from one end of the parking lot to the other. I was amazed how well she could handle the ball without ever touching it with her hands.

"You want me to show you a couple moves?" I asked.

She smiled and shook her head. "Gringos can't play soccer."

"Oh, yeah? How hard can it be?"

She made a gesture with two hands like she was calling me over to her. "Bring it, Cowboy."

We played for a few minutes. She was right. This Gringo couldn't play soccer at all.

"Call me when you think you're better than me," she said.

"That'll be next week."

"Not in our lifetime will you ever be better than me."

"We'll see about that."

"I hope that's true."

As she got in her car to leave, I said, "Thank you, DeAnna, for coming. It's always the best part of my day."

"Mine too, actually."

Maria's husband, Eduardo, still hadn't found a full-time job. Every morning he stood outside a hardware store, waiting for someone to hire him for the day. When there was still snow on the ground, he'd sometimes stand there all day. But as spring came, and lawn and garden work was needed, he began working every day. He'd be hired either by local landscapers or just by people with big yards who wanted work done but didn't want to pay too much for it.

DeAnna told me how proud Eduardo and Maria were to have been able to buy a used car and how grateful she was when they bought the car to use her social security card as proof of her identity.

When people wanted yard work done on Sunday, Eduardo had to quit going to church in the Spanish Branch, but, even so, he still continued to be taught by the missionaries.

I received a letter in May telling me I'd been accepted to Arizona State University. The only thing I still needed before I could for sure go there with DeAnna was an academic scholarship. Because of my high A.C.T. scores, I figured it was a sure thing.

On the second Wednesday in May, just three weeks before high school graduation, DeAnna visited me at work. Even though I had a customer, she came right up to me. "I need to talk to you now. It's really important."

"Excuse me," I said to my customer.

We went outside. "What's up?"

"Maria just called. She said the Feds raided the meat packing plant today. They arrested eleven illegal aliens who worked there."

"What about Maria?"

"When ICE came, they first concentrated on the people doing manual work. She was in the office, so they left her alone, but then her boss and someone from ICE asked her for the files of all the workers. She gave them the files, which had her social security number. Right after that she slipped out the back door. She drove by where Eduardo was working and picked him up. Right now they're at their house packing up. They're leaving town as soon as they can. They probably won't come back here. Can you get away now so you can tell them good-bye?"

I was tending the store alone. "I wish I could, but I can't. There's nobody else here. I'll get fired if I close up early."

"I'll tell her you said good-bye then."

"This means she's not ever going to pay me back, doesn't it?"

"I don't know. Does it really matter?"

"Yes, it matters. Not to me but to my dad. He keeps talking about how stupid I was for loaning her that money. He tells me all the time she'll never pay it back. And now I guess I'll have to tell him he was right all along."

"Is the money all you care about?"

"No. It's just that my dad is on my case all the time about the money. I'll miss Maria and Eduardo and their kids. Tell them that for me, okay?"

"I will."

"I know this is awkward, but could you tell Maria I'd appreciate it if she could still keep trying to repay the money I gave her?"

"I'll do that too."

I shook my head.

"What's wrong?"

"What if they don't pay me back? How can I convince my folks to let me go to Arizona State University instead of BYU-Idaho if I don't have that money in my mission account?"

"Maria and Eduardo will pay you back."

"The one thing I know is that you and I have to be together our freshman year."

"Why?"

"Because I love you."

"Are you sure?"

"Yeah, I'm sure. If we can at least be together our freshman year that will make it easier for me to go on a mission. I don't want to be away from you for three years."

My customer was getting tired of waiting. He came outside where we were talking. "Hey, can I get a little help here?"

"Sorry. I'll be right there," I said.

DeAnna was on her way to her car. "Can you stay here until I take care of him?" I asked.

"No, I need to go," she said.

"Will you please ask Maria to keep sending me money to pay off her loan?"

"Are you sure that's the last thing you want her to hear from you?"

"What do you mean?"

"I would think you'd want her to know how much you admire her for being such a good mom, and for being baptized, and for living the gospel. I would think you would want her kids to know that you love them and you'll miss them. I would think you would want Eduardo to know you hope he will learn to love the Savior."

"Yeah, sorry. Please tell her that, too."

"I will. She will always be grateful to you. And it's one of the reasons I respect you so much."

I watched her leave and then hurried to wait on my customer.

Just before going home from work, I called DeAnna to see if Maria and Eduardo and their two kids were still at their apartment. She told me they had left even before she got back to see them.

"So you didn't get a chance to ask her to keep paying me back?" I asked.

She sighed. "No, sorry, but I'm sure she'll pay you back."

We talked a few more minutes and then she said she had to go.

"I love you," I said.

"I know you do and I love you too." She sighed. "There's something, though, we need to talk about."

"What?"

"We need to let Chad and Jonathan know about, you know, us."

"Yeah, you're right."

"It might be the end of the Four Amigos," she said.

"I know but we have so little time anyway before we graduate. And the Four Amigos probably won't survive after that."

"Probably not."

"I'll tell them Monday during lunch," I said.

"Okay, I'll eat fast and then leave so you can tell 'em."

"Sounds good."

On Monday, in my first period class, I worked it out in my mind what I was going to tell Chad and Jonathan about DeAnna and me.

In my eleven o'clock class, a secretary came to my classroom, walked into the room, and asked, "Is Daniel Winchester here?"

I raised my hand.

"Would you come with me to the office?"

I glanced at the other students and knew they would think I was in some kind of trouble. "Oh," I said for their benefit, "is this for Student of the Year? I am so honored. There are so many others who are much more deserving than me."

I could tell by the secretary's forced smiled that it was something else. And that it wasn't going to be good.

"What is this about?" I asked the secretary as we headed toward the office.

"I was just asked to come and get you."

"Well, can you tell me this? Is there anyone from Immigration and Customs Enforcement in the office?"

She cleared her throat. "Yes, there is, but they just want to talk to you."

"Just a minute. I really need to use the restroom," I said.

"Can't it wait?"

"No, it can't. Please, it will only take a minute."

She nodded, and I ran into the restroom and called my dad and told him what was happening. He told me not to say anything until he and Mr. Farrentino arrived.

I sat down on the counter and waited.

"Are you still in there?" the secretary called out through the closed door.

"Yes. I'm not done yet. It must be something I ate."

Ten minutes later my dad called and said they were on the way and would be at the school in five minutes.

I splashed water on my face to make it look as though I'd been sweating, and came out of the restroom. "Thank you for waiting. I feel much better now."

When we entered the office, the principal was waiting for me in the outer office. "Daniel, we'll be meeting in my office. Follow me."

The door was closed. He opened it and invited me to come in.

Two men in cheap wrinkled suits stood up.

The principal made the introductions. "Daniel, this is Mr. Coulter and Mr. Davenport. They work for the U.S. Immigration and Customs Enforcement, which is commonly called ICE. They are here today to ask you a few questions."

Wearing their dark, cheap-looking, wrinkled suits, they looked like a couple of characters out of an episode of a TV cop show.

"I'm not answering any questions without my lawyer present," I said.

"There's no need for a lawyer," Mr. Coulter said. "We just have a few questions, that's all."

There was a knock on the door, but before anyone could open it, my dad and Mr. Farrentino entered the room.

After more introductions, Mr. Coulter said that it really wasn't necessary to have Mr. Farrentino present. "We just want to ask a few questions."

Mr. Farrentino wasn't buying that. "Let me just say that my purpose here is to protect my client, Daniel Winchester, from self-incrimination, which is, as you know, his right under the Constitution."

"This boy is not a person of interest, but we do believe he can give valuable information that will be helpful in our investigation," Mr. Coulter said. He had a gravelly voice that sounded as though he used sandpaper on it every morning. He was mostly bald except for an oasis of hair near the front that stood up. I couldn't help thinking he looked a little like a cartoon character.

"You can ask whatever question you'd like, but I must inform you that if any of your questions could potentially be incriminating to my client, I will advise him not to answer," Mr. Farrentino said.

"There's no need to make a big deal out of this," Mr. Coulter said. He had a pot belly and dark sunglasses, which he was still wearing. "My first question for you, Daniel, is, do you know a woman named Maria Sanchez?"

I glanced over at Mr. Farrentino who nodded his head. "Yes."

"How did you meet her?"

I didn't want to get Jonathan and Chad involved in this. "When I was asked to deliver a Christmas box to people in our ward."

"Ward? You mean a political district?"

"It's a religious designation, like a parish," Mr. Farrentino said.

"Oh. You may continue," Mr. Coulter said.

So I did. "Well, I delivered the box to the wrong house, and that's how I first met Maria and her two kids."

"I see. And was that your only contact with Maria Sanchez?" Mr. Coulter asked.

"No, I went back several times."

Mr. Coulter was a cut-to-the-chase-kind-of-guy. He removed his sunglasses to make his point. "At the risk of being blunt, did you or did you not have a relationship with this woman?"

"You don't have to answer that question," Mr. Farrentino advised me.

"Answer it? I don't even understand it."

"Did you have a sexual relationship with Maria Sanchez?" Mr. Coulter clarified.

My mouth dropped open. "What?"

Mr. Farrentino stood up. "Daniel, I repeat, you do not have to answer that question."

I looked at Mr. Coulter. "No, I didn't. What a dumb thing to ask."

Now Mr. Coulter was twirling his sunglasses. "If that's true, then I must tell you I'm having a little trouble understanding why you gave this woman over seven hundred dollars over the course of a few days."

"And how do you know that?" Mr. Farrentino shot back.

"We've examined his bank account records."

"Why would you do that?"

"Based on the testimony of two women who worked with Maria Sanchez at the meat packing plant. Maria Sanchez told these women that Daniel Winchester provided money to her so she could obtain a fraudulent social security card. That was all we needed to demonstrate just cause to look at his bank account records."

Mr. Davenport had a cold but apparently had run out of tissues. He kept sniffing to hold back the flow from his runny nose. "Five hundred dollars was withdrawn from your account, Daniel, just a few days before Maria Sanchez, in applying for a job at the meat packing plant, committed identity theft by using her fraudulent social security card."

"Did you pony up all that money without her giving you, shall we say, any favors in return?" Mr. Coulter asked.

"Don't answer the question, Daniel," Mr. Farrentino said.

"Okay, I won't."

"Daniel, were you aware she used money to procure the social security number belonging to a two-year-old boy from Scranton, Pennsylvania?"

I looked at Mr. Farrentino.

"Do not answer that question."

"Then I won't."

"So, in other words, you knew?" Mr. Coulter asked.

"Not the part about Scranton, Pennsylvania."

Mr. Farrentino banged his fist on the table. "If you're not going to answer a question, don't answer any part of the question!"

Mr. Coulter continued. "Are you aware that Maria Sanchez is now a person of interest in an identity theft probe? Not only her but anyone who may have aided her in violating federal laws. Such as yourself. As you've just admitted in front of several witnesses. However, if you cooperate with us, and tell us where Maria Sanchez is now, I will cut you some slack and recommend we not press charges against you."

Mr. Farrentino stood up. "With all due respect, Mr. Coulter, you and I both know you're blowing smoke here. You have no proof that he had any knowledge that any money he may or may not have lent her would be used for illegal purposes."

"We have the sworn statements of two women who attended a religious service wherein Maria Sanchez was baptized. They have told us that at the aforementioned baptism meeting, Maria Sanchez pointed out Daniel Winchester to these coworkers. She told them that he was the one who gave her money so she could procure a fraudulent social security card. Because of this we can make the case that he, with full knowledge, did in effect aid her in this violation of a federal statute."

"If he committed any misdeed, it is simply having a kind heart," Mr. Farrentino argued.

"Look, relax, I'm trying to help the boy. Daniel, do you know where Maria Sanchez is now?" Mr. Coulter asked.

"No, I don't. She didn't say where she was going."

Mr. Coulter nodded. "Just one more question and then we'll let you go back to your class. Was there anyone else involved with you in providing help to Maria Sanchez? If so, I will need their names."

I paused.

"Daniel? Their names?" Mr. Coulter asked again.

I didn't want Chad and Jonathan dragged into this in any way. Even if it meant I had to go to jail.

I sighed and glanced at my dad, who looked like he was going to explode, even though he had said nothing. "No, it was just me. It was my money, nobody else's. And, yes, I knew Maria was going to buy a fake social security card with the five hundred dollars I gave her."

Mr. Farrentino turned to me. "Do you understand what you just did? You just confessed to a federal crime!"

Even Mr. Coulter seemed surprised by my answer. "I see. Well, I appreciate you owning up to that. Given your age and the cooperation you have given us, I will certainly recommend leniency."

I figured I would probably end up in jail, but that would be okay if it spared Chad and Jonathan.

After Mr. Coulter and Mr. Davenport left, Mr. Farrentino railed on me for ten minutes. And then he left. My dad stayed to talk to me. "I think we could have made better use of Mr. Farrentino than we did."

"Sorry."

"I guess we'll just have to see how this all plays out."

"I guess so. Thanks, Dad, for everything."

"One way or the other, we'll get through this," my dad said.

"Yeah, we will, for sure."

"Do you have a minute? I'd like to talk some more."

"I just have lunch now."

"Can I take you to lunch?" he asked.

"Yeah, sure, that'd be great."

We ended up at a restaurant my folks liked. My dad recommended the salad bar because we wouldn't have to wait to get started eating, so that's what I did.

This was new territory to me. I'd never eaten out with just him. "Your mom and I have been talking. She's let me see that I've been unfair to DeAnna and Maria, her husband and their two kids. It wasn't right of me to talk about a family that has just been baptized as a bunch of Mexicans. Also, I had no right to accuse you of picking up a girl off the streets and taking her to a motel for immoral purposes."

"It's okay. I should have told you beforehand what I was doing and why," I said.

My dad continued. "When my grandparents had to sell their store, everyone in the family blamed it on Mexicans who got groceries on credit and never paid them back. But this morning I called and talked to my cousin who still lives down there. He said he thought the reason their store had to close was because of a big grocery store that moved to town about that time. So I'd been told wrong. I apologize to you for being so unfair to you, when all you were trying to do was to help a mom and her two kids, and then, later, her husband."

"Thank you for saying that."

"I love you, Dan."

"I love you too, Dad."

"We'll get through this little problem with Immigration."

"Thanks, Dad."

"They have ice cream. It's free, too."

"Okay, let's have some."

In the car when Dad pulled up to let me off at school, he said, "One thing that's come from this is that I've learned I need to work on changing my attitudes about people from other cultures. You don't, though. You treat all people with dignity and compassion. I'm proud of you for that. I hope I'll be able to catch up with you some day."

I was stunned as I watched him drive off. He'd never treated me like an adult before. As far as I could remember, he had never apologized to me either. I wondered if it was because he realized I might end up in federal prison, and he didn't have much time to mend fences with me.

When I got home from work, I found my room with everything in it, just the way it had been before my dad had emptied it. My mom and dad also told me I could attend the Spanish Branch again. They both said they would like to attend once in a while too.

We had family prayer. My dad asked my mom to say it. Halfway through, she started crying and had to pause for a while. I could tell they were both worried I'd end up in jail. I felt bad for putting them through so much.

After the prayer, we hugged each other, and then I went upstairs to my room and read my patriarchal blessing. It says that some day I will serve in leadership positions in the church. It didn't say I'd go to jail, so I thought that was a good sign.

Maybe some day I'll be a bishop of a prison ward, I thought. As I fell asleep, I was trying to decide if it would be better to have a car thief, a pick pocket, or a bank robber as a counselor.

The next day at school, DeAnna and I told Chad and Jonathan that she and I were officially seeing each other. On Wednesday, in retaliation for Chad's lost pride, he showed up at lunch with a tall blonde cheerleader with the intellect of a cereal box. Her name was Mary Belle, but from the way Chad kept talking about Christmas, it was clear to us that he thought it was Merry Bells. So we started calling her that too.

Merry Bells was what Chad called a hottie. Although he didn't say it, I knew he was just trying to show DeAnna he could get someone better than her. In his mind this was the War of the Bimbos. Not that DeAnna was a bimbo, but Chad would never have been able to pick up on that degree of subtlety.

The reason we liked having Merry Bells eat lunch with us is that if she didn't get one of Chad's jokes (which she seldom did), she'd notice we were laughing, and then she'd laugh, too.

Over the next couple of days Jonathan, DeAnna, and I would start laughing even though what Chad had just said wasn't actually funny. Like if he said he got a C on a test, we'd start laughing, and then Mary Bells would laugh, and that would make us laugh even harder. Even Chad thought that was funny.

We were a very happy table.

By Monday of the next week though, DeAnna told Jonathan and me that she didn't feel good about us treating Merry Bells that way. So we stopped. She also insisted we call her Mary Belle.

Chad wanted Mary Belle to be made an official amigo, so we'd be the Five Amigos. I suggested we go with The Four Amigos plus one Gringo.

"Look who's talking," DeAnna teased.

"*Yo soy un gran hombre hispano,*" I said. I sounded all the H's on purpose. It was such bad Spanish that DeAnna couldn't help laughing. And of course, Mary Belle joined in.

In the end we didn't do anything about the Five Amigos because by then we were only a few weeks from graduating.

On Friday of that week I was called to the office for a phone call. Mr. Coulter of ICE, calling from California, demanded my cooperation in helping them locate Maria and her family. He told me if I didn't help him, he would have me arrested for complicity in identity theft.

He was so arrogant and stupid that I didn't respect him. "Let me ask you something," I said, "is this the biggest case you've got? The reason I ask is there's got to be some actual criminals out there that you could spend your time on."

He swore at me, so I hung up. He called back, but I didn't answer. But then after the fifth call I started to worry I'd make him so mad that he'd fly out here and have me arrested.

So I picked up again.

"Listen, punk, you don't seem to understand the seriousness of your situation. I can make life very hard on you, so I suggest you listen up and give me what I need. Do you understand me?"

"Yes, sir. Sorry."

"Sorry? Sorry doesn't cut it with me! Now I need to find out where Maria Sanchez is. Are you going to cooperate with my investigation or not?"

"Yes, of course, I'll tell you everything I know." That seemed safe enough, since I didn't know where she was.

"Have you had any contact from Maria Sanchez?"

"No, sir, I have not."

"Are you telling me the truth? Because if you're not, you're going to spend the next six months in jail just for lying to me."

"I'm telling you the truth. I haven't heard from her or seen her since you and I first talked."

"You're certain?"

"Yes, sir."

"Will you call me if you hear anything from Maria Sanchez?"

I had no intention of ever telling him where Maria was. "Mr. Coulter, one thing I know for sure and that is I definitely don't want to go to jail."

He seemed to relax. "Then I will expect some cooperation from you."

"Of course you will," I said, meaning that I assumed he would expect some cooperation from me. But he wasn't going to get it.

Apparently he believed I was on his side. But I wasn't. Even if I knew where Maria and Eduardo were, I'd never tell him.

On Saturday DeAnna and I went bowling until eleven and then I took her home. She suggested we go in their backyard and talk. They had a tree swing that her dad had set up when she was little, and we sat together on that, although it was a little cramped.

We talked for a while and then she suggested we go clear in the back of their yard so she could show me their strawberry patch.

When we got back there, she said, "This is our strawberry patch."

It was too dark to see anything, but I said, "Looks good."

She looked at me in a certain way, so I kissed her. Up to then, it was the best thing that had ever happened to me. "Eso fue increible!" I whispered in her ear.

She laughed. "So what do you do, Cowboy, memorize Spanish phrases you hope you'll get lucky enough to use on me some day?"

I laughed. "Yeah, basically."

"Why don't you just take a Spanish class?"

"I will at Arizona State University in the fall."

"I'll take it with you. Good night, Daniel."

"I love you," I said as we left our own private Garden of Eden.

"I love you too."

On Tuesday during lunch, DeAnna handed me a letter addressed to her from Maria. I was surprised that she'd written it in English. From it I learned that she and her family were in California. Eduardo was working on a farm. He'd been baptized a few weeks earlier. She sent me a picture of their family, and they looked very happy—all dressed up in their Sunday best. I was surprised how much Gabriel and Kristina had grown. Maria had written her return address on the envelope, but I tried not to read it

In the letter was a second envelope, and in that envelope there were six hundred dollars in cash. She said this was to help pay me back for what she had borrowed.

"Can you write Maria and ask her not to send me any more money until I contact her again? I don't want ICE getting hold of one of her letters and finding out where she's living."

"If that's what you want, I'll write and tell her to stop sending money and not to write us anymore, until we contact her."

I nodded. "Thanks."

"What are you going to do with the letter?" she asked.

"I'm going to burn it so there's no record of Maria's return address."

She wrote down the address on a scrap of paper. "I'll send the letter and then burn this."

That night I burnt her letter. The next day I reimbursed Jonathan and Chad for their help when we paid Maria's rent. And then I hid the rest of the money in my bedroom because I suspected ICE was still monitoring my bank account. When I told my dad about the money Maria had sent, he apologized again to me for saying she'd never pay me back.

I think I first began loving my dad as a near-adult because he was humble enough to apologize when he could see he'd made a mistake. I hoped I could be like that when I was all grown up.

Three days before graduation Mr. Coulter showed up at school to talk to me. This time they'd given him the use of the guidance counselor's office. He was waiting for me at the door when I entered the office.

"Sit down. I just have a few questions. That's all." He forced a smile, but it looked more like a grimace. "How's school going?"

"Good. Mr. Coulter, I'm wondering if I should call my dad's lawyer, Mr. Farrentino, and ask him to join us."

Mr. Coulter forced a smile and chuckled. "No, that won't be necessary. I just want to see how things are going for you. What are your plans after you graduate?"

"Well, I've been accepted to Arizona State University, so I'll be going there in the fall."

"Really? Well I'm sure that's important to you. And I just hope you'll be able to do that."

I was puzzled. "What do you mean?"

"If I don't start getting some cooperation from you, you'll probably end up in a federal prison in the fall. But that all depends on you. Have you heard from Maria Sanchez?" he asked.

"Yes, I have. She actually wrote me a letter."

"May I see that letter?"

"No, I don't have it anymore."

"What did you do with it?"

"I burnt it." To buy some time, I added, "But, you know what, she'll probably write again."

"The next time she writes, give me the letter. If you do that, all charges against you will be dropped. Do you know where she's living?"

I paused. "Not really. I didn't memorize the address."

"Do you know what state it came from?"

"Well, yeah, I do know that, but I won't tell you."

He stood up. "What do you mean you won't tell me? You want to go to jail?"

"Not really."

Still standing, he leaned toward me and banged his fist on the table. "Then you tell me, and you tell me now!"

"No, I won't."

He banged his fist on the table. "Then you can kiss your freedom goodbye, Buddy Boy! The other prisoners are going to love having a sweet young thing such as yourself. Especially the 300 pound convicted sex offenders."

"Actually, Mr. Coulter, I think my dad's lawyer, Mr. Farrentino, would be very interested in what you just said to me. The way you're speaking to me seems, well, very unprofessional." I stood up and walked out of the office. Mr. Coulter followed me into the hall. He was swearing until one of the secretaries in the office told him there was no need for that kind of language in this school.

I turned to face him. "Mr. Coulter, you said that there was no reason for me to bring Mr. Farrentino in with me. You were wrong. I will never talk to you again without him present or all three of us on a conference call."

He followed me out of the school. As soon as we got outside, he began yelling again. "I am going to bring you down, you little punk!

You can forget about Arizona State, you hear me! Nobody messes with me!"

A school safety officer asked me if he was bothering me. I told him he was.

So the safety officer had a long talk with Mr. Coulter. I wished I could have stayed to see what happened, but I thought it best to just keep walking.

From this experience I decided that I'd like to be the kind of lawyer who would protect people from all the Mr. Coulters in the world who use the law to deny people their rights.

The next day, Mr. Farrentino called Mr. Coulter and demanded the name and phone number of his supervisor. Coulter wouldn't give it to him, so Mr. Farrentino called the regional head of ICE and complained about what he called Coulter's "egregious behavior."

And so for a while Mr. Coulter's "egregious behavior," as Mr. Farrentino described it, became the most important issue.

We were told that a Mr. Hughes would be "assisting" Mr. Coulter. I received an official letter from ICE that required me to inform him of any change in address. There was a form I was to fill out if I contemplated moving. It had to be approved before I moved.

My dad called and asked Mr. Hughes why I had to report any change in address. Mr. Hughes said, "In case we need to get hold of him. If we go to his last listed address and find out he's not there, and we can't locate him, we'll issue an arrest warrant."

"On what basis?"

"Are you serious? We have his confession that he was a party in identity theft. The only reason we haven't gone to court is we're hoping he'll help us. We just need to know where Daniel is living at all times. If he's going to college, just have him fill out the change of address form. That will take care of it. It takes us about two weeks to process. After your son receives a confirmation, then he's free to move."

Because of the cloud of imprisonment facing me, my graduation day wasn't as happy as I'd imagined it would be. Chad had a party at his house. About two in the morning everyone left except the Four Amigos. We drove out of town to a campsite and made a fire and made s'mores and talked until dawn. And then we went in the back of Jonathan's house and lay down on the trampoline and we all fell asleep. I woke up at ten, kissed DeAnna on the cheek and walked home and went to bed until two in the afternoon.

It wasn't much different being a high school graduate. I still worked at the same place most of the summer, but at the beginning of August, because I was about to begin as a freshman at Arizona State University, I quit my job. My mom and dad and I went on a two week family vacation. We toured church history sites in New York, Ohio, and Illinois, and along the way we visited my brother Kevin and his wife and two kids in Detroit.

"A year from now, you'll be submitting your mission papers," my mom said as we were walking in the Sacred Grove in Palmyra. Even though it was shady, it was still very hot and humid. But it was also very peaceful and quiet in the shade of the trees. "We wanted you to see all this before your mission. Besides, after your mission, you won't be spending much time with us anymore." She gave me a hug. "So I can see all this is coming to a close."

My dad suggested we have a prayer while we were in the Sacred Grove. We found a bench to sit on. We waited until nobody was around and then my dad began to pray.

During the prayer my cell phone rang. My mom sighed. She hated cell phones. She had quietly fumed as DeAnna and I texted through most of our vacation.

"Can you turn it off?" she asked.

"Yeah, sure." I did that and my dad continued his prayer. He talked about me going away for college and about my mission and asked for blessings for me to honor my priesthood.

After he finished, we hugged each other and then started back to our car.

I turned on my cell phone. The call I'd missed was from DeAnna. She'd also sent me a text message that said, "Call me."

So I called her. When she picked up, she sounded stressed.

"What are you doing?" I asked.

"There's somebody here who wants to talk to you."

Mr. Coulter came on the line. "Where are you?"

"New York."

"You think you can hide in New York, is that what you think? You little punk."

"I'm on vacation with my mom and dad."

"I don't care about that! I told you to stay put! Yesterday I came to town to check up on you. I called your home number and there was no answer. I went to your employer and he told me you'd quit your job and left town. What was I to think except that you were on the run to avoid prosecution? Well, you're not going to get away with this! I'll have you in jail for the rest of your life. Nobody crosses me! Nobody makes me look bad to my superiors! Tell me where you are so I can have you arrested!"

"You know what? Let me get back to you. I need to speak with our lawyer."

He started swearing at me. "If you hang up on me, I will have your girlfriend DeAnna here jailed as a material witness."

"You seem a little upset, Mr. Coulter. Why is that?" I asked.

While he went on another tirade, I told my dad what was happening. He used his cell phone to call Mr. Farrentino and tell him what the situation was.

I stayed on the line with Mr. Coulter, doing my best to give him the impression I wanted to work with him by occasionally adding, "I can see why that would make you mad, Mr. Coulter."

Finally my dad finished his conversation with our lawyer. "Mr.

Farrentino is going to call him and work out a compromise," he told me.

"Can he have me arrested?"

My dad sighed. "Yeah, he can. You did confess to identity theft. It's not a strong case, but he can keep this tied up for a long time. Mr. Farrentino will see if he can work out a compromise."

I returned to Mr. Coulter. "Mr. Farrentino, my attorney, should be calling you any minute to work out a compromise. So we'll see you around, okay?"

"Stay where you are. If you move, I'll have you arrested for flight to avoid arrest. Do you understand me?"

"We'll stay here until we hear from Mr. Farrentino."

And so we stayed. The Sacred Grove, instead of a place of peace and reverence became for us almost a prison.

At nine thirty our time, Mr. Farrentino called my dad. The compromise he'd worked out was that we could continue our vacation but, once we got back home, I was not to leave town until they decided if ICE wanted to take my case to trial.

"How long will that be?" I asked.

"It could be as much as a year or two," he said.

"But what about my plans to go to Arizona State University in the fall?" I asked.

"That will have to be put on hold."

"And what about me serving a mission for my church?"

"Same thing. Nothing can happen until ICE makes a decision of what they want to do."

"That's not fair."

"Probably not, but that's the way it is. You confessed to identity theft. It would be a slam dunk case for them. It's almost too tempting for them not to pursue it."

"I can't believe this is happening to me."

"There's one other thing. Mr. Coulter wants you to understand that if you were to decide to take off on the run, he would have

DeAnna arrested as a material witness. So if you want her to stay out of jail, you need to do what ICE tells you to do."

Suddenly my world had been turned upside down. And it had happened in the Sacred Grove.

Chapter Ten

We got home from our vacation five days later, about ten thirty at night. I called DeAnna and asked if I could come over. She said yes. My mom suggested it would be better to wait until morning, but I told her I had to see DeAnna.

When she came to the door, I could tell she was still mad at me for the ordeal she'd gone through with Mr. Coulter. He threatened her with jail time too because she admitted to him that Maria had sent her a letter for me, which in his mind made her an accessory to the crime of identity theft.

We went out to the strawberry patch. I held her in my arms while she told me every detail of Mr. Coulter's visit. I told her over and over again how sorry I was she got dragged into this.

"I keep having nightmares about being in prison. My mom and dad are scared too."

"I'm so sorry."

"What are you going to do?" she asked.

"Stay in town. I can't risk being arrested."

"So we won't be together at school in Arizona?"

"Not until this blows over."

"And what about your mission?"

"I'll just have to wait until my lawyer works this out. But, you know what? At least I have a lawyer. The ones I feel sorry for are the people who don't."

Her dad came into the back yard. "DeAnna?" he called out.

"Yes."

"Are you still with Daniel?"

"Yes."

"I want to talk to the two of you inside."

We followed him inside.

He sat us down in his office. "All I've ever wanted for DeAnna is that she have the opportunities I never had. I want her to receive a college education. I want her to marry a fine young man who has a good education too. We've always hoped she would marry a returned missionary who honors his priesthood. We do not want anything to get in the way of our hopes and dreams for her. And right now you could be someone who could put an end to the dreams we have for our daughter."

"I want her to have those same things too."

"You're not going to Arizona State University in the fall, are you?"

"No."

"I am sorry to hear that. But, even so, I would appreciate you encouraging her to go to college in Arizona like she's planned. Just because you won't be going doesn't mean she shouldn't."

"I agree."

"I'll tell you what worries me the most. And that would be if you two get married and she gets pregnant and then you get sent to prison, leaving my daughter with a child and no husband around to help her. I do not want that to happen."

"We'll be sure that doesn't happen," she said.

"I hope you will both remember this talk and what you promised me."

"We will."

"I know you're both living the Gospel, but be careful. No more sneaking into our backyard. Daniel, if you're going to kiss my daughter, I suggest you kiss her at the door, just before you leave us."

"Okay."

"Fine, then, that is all I have to say." He stood up and left.

"I am so embarrassed," DeAnna said softly to me. "It's like he doesn't trust us."

"It's okay. He's just looking out for you."

"I know."

I never knew if it was because of her dad talking to me the way he did, or if it was just the slow realization that our paths were about to diverge, but from then on we weren't as close as we'd been. With each passing day, I wanted to spend more time with her, but it seemed we spent less. She quit talking about how excited she was to begin at Arizona State because she knew how painful it was to me.

I wanted her to stay in town with me but the few times I brought it up, she accused me of only thinking of myself.

It seemed like every day brought a new disappointment. I didn't have any luck getting a new job so I stayed with my old one working the same hours I'd had in high school.

My dad encouraged me to take classes at our local community college. To call it a college wasn't quite accurate. It was one building consisting of three class rooms. The course choice was limited. I signed up for a course that taught how to use Excel spread sheet software. It was a night class. Twenty people signed up but they only had ten computers in the classroom so two people were assigned a computer. My partner was a retired dentist who was only taking the course because his wife told him he had to get out of the house once in a while because he was driving her crazy. I soon discovered why.

I also signed up for a beginning Spanish course taught by a guy my age whose only credentials was he'd taken the course the previous semester. I had to keep correcting the way he pronounced the words.

Finally it came down to the day before DeAnna and her folks were to drive her to Tempe for college. I helped her carry boxes of what she was taking out to the family car.

We ate lunch in her backyard.

"I'll miss you," she said.

"I know. Me too."

"We'll call and text, though," she said.

"Yeah, we will."

"Do you need any money? I could give you five hundred dollars," I said.

"Why would you do that?"

"It's from the money Maria sent me to pay me back. I don't have any use for it now."

"I'm okay. Thank you though."

"There wouldn't be any record of it, if that's what you're worrying about, because I didn't put it in the bank, you know, because ICE is probably monitoring my bank account, so it'd be okay for you to have it."

"Will you ever be out from under this burden?" she asked.

"I don't know. Maybe not. Even if they don't do anything, there's always the possibility that they could. This could go on for years."

"Dan, I think what we've shared is what they call true love," she said.

"I think so too."

"The world doesn't like true love because it reminds everyone else how much they've been cheated."

"It will turn out. Eventually it will all work out."

"Let's always keep that hope in our hearts," she said.

She stood up. "Would you like to help me carry one last box from my room?"

"Yes, of course."

I followed her up the stairs to her room. Once we were both inside, she closed the door.

"Oh, Dan," she said with tears in her eyes. "I love you. I'm going to miss you so much."

"I know. Me too."

She started crying.

I put my arms around her and held her as she sobbed.

A short time later we heard the garage door open and a car drive in. She sighed. "It's my mom. She's back from her errands. Could you take this box downstairs and put it in the back with all the others?"

"Yes, of course."

"That's the last box, Dan. You won't need to come up here anymore."

"I understand."

A short time later DeAnna's father came home. He didn't like the way I'd packed the SUV so I helped him re-pack it. And then Domino's delivered pizza and they asked me to stay and have dinner with them. I stayed until nine and then DeAnna said she had some things she needed to do, so I gave her a hug and went home.

Later I called and asked when they were leaving in the morning. She said six so I set my alarm.

The next morning at quarter to six I rang her doorbell several times but nobody answered. I went out to the garage and looked through a small window and saw that the SUV had gone.

They left earlier. She texted me later in the day and said she couldn't face having to leave me. We texted most of the day.

Chad and Jonathan left the next day for BYU in Provo.

"It's not like we won't see each other again. We'll come home probably every other weekend," Chad said.

The truth was the only time they came home was for Thanksgiving and Christmas.

Once DeAnna was set up in her dorm room, we switched from

texting to Instant Messenger communications. Her name was DeAnna23. Mine was Cowboy92.

This was the one I remember the most.

> *DeAnna 23: I'll be busy tomorrow night.*
>
> *Cowboy92: What will you be doing?*
>
> *DeAnna23: A guy from my institute class invited me to a dance.*
>
> *Cowboy92: What's his name?*
>
> *DeAnna23: Quentin.*
>
> *Cowboy92: Sounds more like a medicine than a name.*
>
> *DeAnna23: LOL*
>
> *Cowboy92: Returned missionary?*
>
> *DeAnna23: Yes. He served in Chile. He speaks fluent Spanish. And he likes to practice his Spanish with me.*
>
> *Cowboy92: Yes, I bet he does. Is he practicing anything else with you?*
>
> *DeAnna23: What do you think?*
>
> *Cowboy92: Sorry. How long has he been back from his mission?*
>
> *DeAnna23: Two years.*
>
> *Cowboy92: So he's probably ready to get married, right?*
>
> *DeAnna23: I have no idea. The point is I'm not.*
>
> *Cowboy92: We never talked about seeing other people while you were gone.*
>
> *DeAnna23: That's because we both realized it was going to happen.*
>
> *Cowboy92: I haven't dated anyone since you left.*

DeAnna23: It's only been two days. And, actually, you should.

Cowboy92: Why, so you won't feel guilty?

DeAnna23: Last I checked we're not engaged. You've got a mission ahead of you.

Cowboy92: Not if ICE has its way.

DeAnna23: You saying if I can't serve a mission I might as well marry DeAnna.

Cowboy92: You're the one who talks about true love all the time.

DeAnna23: If you love me you should want the best for me.

Cowboy92: I just don't want you stolen away from me.

DeAnna23;I'M NOT YOUR PROPERTY SO I CAN'T BE STOLEN!

Cowboy92: You know what I mean.

DeAnna23: You should see other girls while I'm gone.

Cowboy92: What other girls? The only eligible female in my Excel course is the teacher and she's a 32 year old single mom with two kids.

DeAnna23: Maybe she'd give you extra credit if you took her out.

Cowboy92: I don't need extra credit!

DeAnna23 : I know. What about Jonathan's sister Michelle? She used to have a crush on you, right?

Cowboy92: That was a long time ago. Besides, she's still in high school.

DeAnna23: So what? You were in high school last year. She might appreciate a more mature guy like you.

Cowboy92: The girl I want to be with is you.

DeAnna23: Then get in your car and come out here.

Cowboy92: You know I can't do that.

DeAnna23: Then find a substitute. I'm going to date other guys. The more the better, right? If I go out with a different guy every weekend, then you don't have anything to worry about. I'm just saying you should do the same.

Cowboy92: I'll think about it.

DeAnna23: Good. Well, I got to go study. Love you.

Cowboy92: Love you back.

Because I was a few months older than either Chad or Jonathan, I turned nineteen in November. My bishop called me in and we talked about a mission even though he knew about my troubles with ICE and the restriction I stay at home.

"Have you ever thought about serving a mission here? The call would be issued from the stake presidency and you could serve here until you're able to fulfill a full time mission. The time you serve could fit in with your work schedule and other commitments."

"What would I do?"

"Well, I've asked around and you could serve at Deseret Industries and also as a family history missionary. They both need people to help out."

I shook my head. "I don't think so."

"You'd be set apart like any other missionary, and you'd get a name tag to wear while you're serving."

I sighed and shook my head.

"What's wrong?"

"People would make fun of me."

"So what if they do? You'd be serving Father in Heaven. He wouldn't make fun of you. And there would be blessings that would come from your service."

"What kind of blessings?" I asked.

"I'm not sure. I just know Father in Heaven delights to honor those who serve him. Let's just turn to Doctrine and Covenants 76 and read verses 5 and 6."

"I'll take your word, okay? Look, I don't want to be one of those pathetic people who serve at DI."

"Those pathetic people, as you say, have a great deal they could teach you. If you will do this, it will be a great blesssing to you for the rest of your life."

"Let me think about it, okay?"

I went home and told my mom and dad about the bishop's suggestion. They were for it. I was against. We got in an argument and I drove off in my car.

At first I just wanted to drive to try to cool down.

An hour later I found myself on I-15 heading south on my way to Tempe, Arizona to see DeAnna.

At eleven thirty my dad called. "Where are you?"

"Just outside Cedar City."

"Where are you headed?"

"Tempe, to see DeAnna."

"You know that you can't do that! They'll arrest you."

"How can you say that? Have they ever caught Maria and her family? No, they have not. She can go anywhere they want and nobody arrests them. And it's not just them. Why is it that ten million illegal aliens can go wherever they want and never get arrested? So what does ICE do? It focuses all their attention on me. I'm a citizen of this country but they treat me like I'm the illegal alien! Well, I'm sick of it! I need to be with DeAnna. Right now she's the only thing in my life I even care about."

"They'll arrest you because you leave a record wherever you go. When you use your credit card to get gas. Whatever you do, you leave a record. They know your license number. They're probably listening in to this conversation. You've got to turn back before it's too late."

I looked at my gas gauge. I would need to get gas in a couple of hours. I didn't have any cash. All I had was my credit card.

"This isn't fair."

"No, it isn't. I absolutely agree. But don't give up. Mr. Farrentino says he thinks that within a few months he'll be able to get this resolved. He's been talking with a staff member of Senator Ashworth, and he thinks the senator will be able to apply pressure to ICE to leave you alone. But none of that will work if you've been arrested and tried and found guilty of assisting in identity theft. So just be patient. Come back here and let us work this out together as a family."

I told him I'd think about it.

At the next exit I took a side road and drove until I came to a place where I could pull off. I got out of my car and stood and looked at the stars.

I started to call DeAnna but then I realized she'd be on her date with the returned missionary and if I called, she'd either not pick up or else tell me she couldn't talk to me and that would be it.

I looked at the stars. "Father in Heaven, do you even care how much my life sucks right now?"

I got nothing except maybe one shooting star, but they happen all the time so it'd be wrong to say that was my answer.

In the end I guess my answer, which took another hour to arrive at, was that my dad was right.

I drove back home and went to bed.

On Sunday I met with my bishop and told him I would accept a call to serve as a missionary, both at Deseret Industries ten hours a week and at the Family History Center ten hours a week. I would continue my job at the plumbing contractor's store and, also, I would be allowed to go on dates. Plus, I got a missionary badge which I was to wear when I was serving at the two places.

The next Sunday I was set apart by our stake president. I thought it would basically be a formality, and that the setting apart would take at most maybe a couple of minutes. I mean, after all, a stake president has lots of better things to worry about than me, right? And that this wasn't really a mission, and God wouldn't want to be giving a lot of blessings for serving a mission where you didn't leave home or even quit your job.

So I was surprised at the blessings promised me if I would serve faithfully. My mom took notes so I could look back on the blessing when I was discouraged.

When I finished, I wiped my face with the sleeve of my suit which of course caused my mom to flinch, but I couldn't let our stake president see me choked up.

During the week I began working. Monday, Wednesday, Friday at the family history library, and Tuesday, Thursday and Saturday at Deseret Industries. I was surprised how friendly and helpful everyone was. On my first day at DI I had a Down Syndrome brother training me on my duties. He did an excellent job and was able to answer all my questions.

Sometimes we make fun of people, but one thing I learned is that God never makes fun of anyone, that he loves them all, everyone. I know that's what we say sometimes but I think none of us really believe it totally. But it's true.

On Sunday, in our sacrament meeting, our bishop invited me to sit on the stand with him. After the opening prayer, he had me stand next to him, wearing my missionary badge. He explained what my mission would be.

I noticed Michelle's mocking grin. She turned to one of her friends and started whispering, I suppose, about me.

It was okay, though. Two of my friends from Deseret Industries had come to listen to my short talk. Later they told me I'd done a good job. So that made me feel good.

Because I served during the day as a missionary, I switched my classes to night classes. The trouble with night classes was that anyone could take them. Like the woman in a computer class who could never remember from week to week how to turn off the computer.

"You go to Start," the teacher would say.

"You want me to go to Start to stop the computer?"

"Yes, that's right."

"Isn't there like an on-off switch?"

"Well, yes, but if you want to save what you've done you have to go through a certain procedure."

"Why would I want to save what I've done? I don't even know what I've done."

"Please go to Start and I'll help you from there."

I began to feel that my role in the class was to keep the instructor from going crazy.

Jonathan and Chad came home for Thanksgiving but DeAnna did not. She said her mom and dad told her it was too expensive and too far to travel just for a couple of days.

They visited me while I was working at the Deseret Industries store. They brought Michelle with them.

My assignment that day was to be the greeter. "Welcome to Deseret Industries," I said.

"Yeah, sure," Chad said. He looked at my name tag. "So, they call this a mission?"

"Yeah, they do. I do too actually."

"So what do you do all day?"

"Well, I greet people, and then I also go in the back room and sort out the clothes people have donated. If you want, I can take you back there."

"No, that's okay. Well, keep up the good work."

Michelle wouldn't even look at me.

"Hello, Michelle," I said.

"How can you do this?" she asked.

"I was called by God."

She scoffed. "Yeah, right. What about the old men at Walmart who are greeters? Are they called by God, too? You're doing the same thing they do. Except they get paid."

Jonathan came to my rescue. "Michelle, there's no reason to talk to him like that."

"Why not? Everyone I know makes fun of him."

Chad turned to Michelle. "You two should go out sometime. You can do that, right, Cowboy? I mean you don't have the same rules as real missionaries, right?"

"That's right."

"I wouldn't be seen with Cowboy if he was the last guy on the planet," Michelle said. "What you're doing here is a joke."

My face turned a bright red. "Can I help you find anything?" I asked.

"You think I shop here for my clothes?" Michelle asked. "Let's get out of here."

"Well, we'd better be going," Chad said.

Jonathan opened the door for Michelle. "We'll be in the car," Jonathan said. And then they left.

"Oh, one thing, Johnny B and I are going to be interviewed for our mission on Sunday," Chad told me.

"That's great," I said.

"Yeah, we're hoping we can go in May, hopefully speak in sacrament the same Sunday. That way I won't have to prepare a long talk. Let's get together sometime and we'll tell you all about BYU. Especially the chicks!"

"Yeah, that'd be great."

"Give me a call."

I didn't call, and by Sunday night they'd gone back to Provo. So much for friends, right?

Chapter Eleven

Sometimes, late at night when I couldn't sleep, I kept playing the story of the Good Samaritan over and over in my mind, wanting to call out to him to leave the bruised and bloody traveler on the ground. I wanted to tell him, "Just keep walking. Don't stop to help him. Just mind your own business. You don't know where this might lead. Don't do it. Just leave him to die. It's not your problem. There are agencies that take care of things like this."

In high school I was a promising student. Somewhere along the way I managed to lose whatever future I might have had. And now I was afraid I might never get it back. I had no interest in the classes I was taking at the community college, and, even worse, I wasn't sure they would even transfer if I was ever able to attend a real university. I felt embarrassed to wear my mission badge because everyone knew I should be serving a real mission away from home.

DeAnna was going out with random guys nearly every weekend, and yet, even though she encouraged me to date, I couldn't think of anyone who would accept a date with me.

A week after Thanksgiving, she called me late at night. She was in tears because a guy she'd been with had touched her inappropriately.

She yelled at him to stop and then called her aunt to come get her.

I listened while she told me all about it. "I'm so sorry you had that happen to you."

"There is nobody out here with any integrity. I miss you so much. I wish you could be here with me all the time."

"Me too."

"I'm never going to find anyone like you."

"You will. Just keep looking," I said with a sigh.

"Why do you say that? Are you not as interested in me as you used to be?"

"I am, it's just that, let's face it, DeAnna, I'm a loser."

"You are not. How can you say that?"

"Everyone else is moving ahead, but I'm stuck here."

"That's only for a little while and then things will get better."

"I don't think so."

"I still love you," she said.

"I don't see why."

"It's because of who you are."

"I'm nothing. Ask anyone. Ask Chad. Ask Jonathan. Ask Michelle. Ask the ones I went to high school with who come into DI. You should see the smirks on their faces when they see me working there."

"You know what? I won't go back to school after Christmas. I'll stay in town with you."

"Your mom and dad won't let you do that. They want you to get a college education."

"And I will. After you're on your mission. I just want to be able to see you every day."

"I'd like that very much too."

"That's what we'll do then."

The hope she was going to come back after Christmas and stay in town got me through the next week until she called to tell me her parents wanted her to finish her freshman year. "They want me to stay here until June. And then I can decide what I want to do after that."

So that dream vanished, too, like all the others.

But the one thing that kept me more upbeat was that DeAnna was at least going to spend two weeks in town during her Christmas break.

I made plans with her and her folks to pick her up at the airport myself. Her flight was scheduled to land at eight that night.

I worked at DI until five which gave me plenty of time to go home, shower, get ready and be at the airport half an hour early, just in case her flight was early.

At quarter to five two men entered the store, asked where I was, came up to me. "Daniel Winchester, you're under arrest for the charge of identity theft."

They handcuffed me and led me out of the store, put me in their car and drove out of town.

They turned onto a side road. We went about half a mile and then they stopped. There was another car parked there.

Mr. Coulter got out of the other car and came over to us. He got in the back seat with me.

The two other men walked to the other car.

Mr. Coulter got in my face. "I want the address of Maria and Eduardo Sanchez, and I want it now. If you won't give it to me, we're going to put you in jail until your trial. You'll get at least five years in a federal prison. So give me what I want."

"I don't have her address."

"Don't give me that! You cooperate or face the consequences! You see what happens when you don't show me the proper respect? You see what happens when you don't cooperate with me? You think this will ever stop? Well it won't. You want to know why? Because I won't let it stop! This isn't about the law! This is about you not giving me the proper respect! That's what it's about! I deserve respect! Especially from some punk kid like you!" And then he began swearing at me.

"You can't do this to me," I said, trying to be calm.

"I can do anything I want! I am the law! And don't you ever forget it!"

One of the other men came over and opened the car door and spoke to Mr. Coulter. "You've gone too far. From now on, you're on your own. We're not risking our jobs for you."

Mr. Coulter's jaw clamped shut and he glared at me, but then nodded. "Okay."

He smiled at me. "If you'll promise not to tell your lawyer about this, I'll let you go. Otherwise I'll have you flown to Denver where you'll be booked for identity theft."

"I can't make that promise."

"What do you mean you can't? I have the power to throw you in jail."

"I want to talk to my lawyer."

"Forget your lawyer! I'm the one you have to deal with, so don't cross me."

"I want to talk to my lawyer."

"Get out of the car! You can walk home for all I care."

Mr. Coulter got in his car and drove away. The other two men apologized for his behavior and drove me home. They told me Mr. Coulter was not doing well lately.

By the time I got home, it was past time for me to leave to pick up DeAnna.

I jumped in my car and drove as fast as I could to the airport. Unfortunately I arrived twenty minutes after the plane had landed.

By the time I arrived at baggage claim DeAnna was standing there all alone, looking abandoned.

"I'm so sorry!" I said.

She was almost in tears. "I looked all around for you, but you weren't there. Nobody came to pick me up. It was like nobody cared."

"ICE picked me up just before I should have left to come get you."

"What did they want?"

"Maria's address."

"Did you give it to them?"

"No, of course not. That's why I was late."

"I was about to call my mom and dad and ask them to come get me."

"I'm really sorry."

"I know." And then she added, "You're always sorry."

A few minutes later I threw her bag into the trunk of my car and opened the car door for her.

I started the car, and then looked at her. "You look real good," I said.

"Thanks."

I apologized again. She told me in great detail how awful it was to realize that nobody was there to pick her up. I told her how bad I felt. And that seemed to help.

And then, without any discussion, we started kissing.

A few minutes later, she put her index finger on my lips. "That's enough for now, don't you think?"

"I guess."

"Take me home before my folks wonder what happened to me."

"Yeah, sure."

After I'd paid the parking fee and pulled onto the street, she asked, "So, if you're on a mission, why were we kissing?"

"I'm not on a mission all the time. I mean, for example, I still work at my same job, and I'm taking a class, and I can date if I want."

"I see. So it's not . . . you know . . . like other missions then, is it?"

"No, not really."

"I've always said I would marry a returned missionary, but I wasn't thinking about this kind of a mission, where sometimes you're on a mission, and sometimes you're not."

That made me mad. "It's the best I can do now, okay?" I grumbled.

"I know. It's great you're serving. You know what? I've missed you so much."

"Me too. More than I could tell you. I was afraid if I told you everything, you'd think I was pathetic."

"I would never think that about you."

We pulled into her driveway. I was hoping for one more kiss before we went inside but her mom and dad saw us and came out running. They threw their arms around her and hugged her.

I stayed until eleven and then went home.

Two days later we drove twenty miles to the grade school where my grandfather worked as the school custodian. I'd made arrangements with a custodian to show us around.

His name was Ethan and he'd only worked there for two years, so he hadn't known my grandfather. He took us to a small room on the first floor where they kept their equipment. "This is where we hang out," he said.

I walked around, looking carefully at the mops and buckets and buffers.

There was a small battered desk and chair that looked like it had been there for many years.

I sat down in the chair. "Maybe my grandfather used to sit here," I said.

Ethan nodded. "Could be. It's been around for a long time."

"My grandfather started working here when he was thirty-six years old. He worked here until he was sixty-one. That's when he got sick. He died when I was three years old. I don't remember anything about him. But he left me some money that he wanted me to use for my mission. I've become very interested in his life. I wish he'd kept a journal but nobody's ever found one. I would like to know what he was like. My mom says he was very much loved by the students and that when they had a problem, many of them would come to him. That's about all I know about him."

"Sorry I can't help you."

"It's okay. Just being here gives me a little more connection with him."

I stood up. "I did something once that if he'd been alive, would have disappointed him very much. I wish I could tell him I'm sorry."

"You can," DeAnna said.

"Yeah, yeah, I know, like I could ask God to tell him I'm sorry. But, you know what, it's not the same."

I stretched out my hand and ran my fingers over the broom that looked the oldest and wondered if my grandfather pushing that broom around the school had made the handle become so worn.

Ethan must have sensed what I was thinking. "You want to keep the broom? We've just got in some new ones. We'd eventually throw this one away anyway."

"Really? That would be great!"

The broom ended up in my room. I hung it on the wall like it was a painting.

Christmas break was great for DeAnna and me. We spent every day together. She dropped into DI while I was working. I showed her around and introduced her to everybody. They treated her like royalty. She also visited the family history center while I was working.

Over the next two weeks she and I went bowling several times, had three or four game nights with Chad and Jonathan, went snow boarding once, and ice skating a couple of times.

On one Sunday we went to the Spanish Branch for church. It was great being with them. Nobody seemed to know much about where Maria, Eduardo and her two kids were living.

She and I went to the stake New Year's Eve dance. We loved dancing together, especially the slow dances.

Two days later she left for Arizona.

And I was left all alone once again.

AT FIRST I had great hope for the way things would turn out for DeAnna and me. Mr. Farrentino was hopeful, in light of Mr. Coulter's treatment of me and others, and his subsequently being forced to choose early retirement, that all charges against me would be dropped.

But as the days slipped by, things changed between DeAnna and me.

She started spending a lot of time with the 24-year-old returned missionary named Quentin who had one more semester before he graduated from college. We quit instant messaging but she did send me an e-mail every few days, telling me mostly about her classes.

And then one day she called and told me that Quentin had proposed to her.

"What did you tell him?" Even as I said it, I had already decided she'd probably end up marrying him because he, at least, had a future.

"I told him it was too soon. I told him all about us. So he knows how I feel about you."

"You like him though, don't you?"

"He's very thoughtful of me."

"I'm sure he is."

"As soon as all charges are dropped against me, I'll come out and spend some time with you. I might even get a job and live out there. So if you could just hold on for a little longer."

"I will. I'm not rushing into anything. My dad wants me to finish college before I get married."

"He's such a wise man," I joked.

She chuckled. "I thought you might say something like that."

As time went on, I didn't hear much from her. I knew that wasn't a good sign.

Even though Mr. Coulter had chosen early retirement, I still wasn't off the hook. Weeks slipped by with no change in my status.

On the second Sunday in February, Chad, recently called to serve a mission in Mexico and Jonathan, called to serve a Spanish-speaking mission in Guatemala, gave talks in sacrament meeting just a few days before they both entered the MTC. DeAnna had flown in for the occasion. I'd paid for the ticket from the money Maria had sent to pay me back.

They gave good talks. I was impressed how much Chad had matured since high school. Jonathan had always been mature but now I sensed his love for teaching the Gospel.

After church, all of our friends from high school had lunch at Jonathan's house.

DeAnna wanted to take a picture of the three of us. She coaxed me into going home and getting my mission badge so she could take it with the three of us as missionaries.

After she took the picture, Michelle sang out, "One of these elders is not like the other, one of these elders just doesn't belong. Guess which one?" she asked.

"I think they all belong," DeAnna said.

"Not the greeter for DI," she said. "He doesn't belong."

"Michelle, this is a real calling," DeAnna said.

"Not really. This was just a consolation prize because he couldn't serve a real mission."

I tore off my mission name tag and started to leave.

DeAnna caught up with me. "Don't you dare leave!"

We were on the sidewalk, halfway between Jonathan's and my house.

"Michelle is right. I don't belong."

"If Father in Heaven appreciates your service, what do you care what anyone else thinks? Come back to the house with me. Let's go back and eat like the wind."

She put her arm around my waist as we walked back. She made everything better for me.

But she left the next day. Back to Quentin and his amazing technicolor proposal.

TWO WEEKS LATER I still hadn't heard from DeAnna about what she'd decided to do about Quentin's proposal of marriage. Mr. Farrentino said he'd hit a roadblock in his efforts to get all charges dropped against me. My classes at the community college were so bad I got a headache every time I went to class.

Another week passed and then DeAnna called me. She told me that Quentin had taken a job in London, England, and that he'd be leaving the end of May. "He wants me to go with him. He'll pay for my education. We would be getting married three weeks before he has to report to work. We'd have our honeymoon in Europe."

"Congratulations," I said.

"I haven't told him yes yet."

"But you will. You know you will. It's just a matter of time. You're just trying to let me down easy. But, look, it's okay, I'm used to things not working out for me."

"I'm not sure I will say yes. He's nice and everything, but he's not you."

"I have nothing to offer you. I haven't served a mission. I don't have a college education. I have no job prospects. I will probably never go to Europe. I'll never make the kind of money he will. My advice is to take his offer."

"I would except for one thing." she said.

"What's that?"

"I still love you."

"You do?"

"I do."

"Then don't marry Quentin," I said.

"Good point. I just wish you could come here."

"Yeah, me too. I wish a lot of things, actually."

"Thank you. I appreciate that."

For the next few days, I was depressed about how little control

I had in my life. I also regretted ever having helped Maria. It seemed to me that all my problems began with that.

One day my dad asked me to take his car to the dealer to have it fixed. They said it would only be half an hour so I decided to wait.

After a few minutes I noticed a woman with a baby in her arms. She was in the process of paying for the repairs to her car.

"That'll be one hundred and thirty seven dollars," the woman behind the counter said.

"No, that's too much. They told me ninety."

"They found some other things that needed to be fixed."

The young mother pulled out some cash from her pocket and began to count it out. "That's ninety dollars. That's all I've got. And I don't have any credit cards."

"I'm sorry, but the bill is one hundred and thirty seven dollars. If you'd like to go home and get some more money, we'll just keep the car here until you get back."

The mom panicked. "Don't you see? I don't have any more money at home! This is all I've got. You've got to help me. My husband is serving in Iraq. That's got to count for something."

"Well, of course it does. All I'm saying is you'll have to talk to our manager. He's out of town for the rest of the week, but he'll be back on Tuesday. We can keep your car until then."

I sat there barely able to breathe, looking around at the other three people waiting for their car to be done.

"We could help her," I said quietly to the woman next to me.

"What?"

"We could all chip in a little, and help that woman pay for her repairs."

The woman shook her head and went back to watching TV.

I sat down next to a man. "We need to help this woman. She doesn't have enough money to pay her bill."

"Do I look rich to you?"

"No."

"Then do I look stupid to you?"

"No, you just look uncharitable."

He told me to go to a place which members of the church would call spirit prison.

I approached the last customer in the waiting room, a woman playing with her Blackberry. Very professional looking. Maybe ten years older than me. Must have had a fine education. She looked up from texting long enough to glare at me. "Don't even think about it."

I stood up and addressed them all. "What is the matter with you people?" I called out.

They ignored me and my question.

I started toward the counter just as an old man walked into the waiting room and sat down.

I stood next to the young mom and her baby and spoke to the clerk. "If you'll knock the bill down ten dollars, I'll pay the balance of what this woman owes."

The clerk pursed her lips. "That's very generous, but you know what? I don't have the authority to reduce someone's bill. You can wait until Tuesday, though, and talk to our manager."

"Look, this woman needs her car. Okay, I'll pay the forty seven dollars." I wrote out a check and handed it to the woman behind the counter.

"Why are you doing this for me?" the young mother asked.

Good question. One I had to think about for a while. Why does a guy with no future go out of his way for a stranger? It was a question that never goes away. It's as old as the Good Samaritan story.

I shrugged. "I don't know. I guess it's just because . . . that's who I am . . . and this is what I do."

The woman had tears in her eyes. "I can't begin to thank you. Things have been so tough for us lately."

"I know. Look, it's okay. You help someone out some day."

"I will." She touched my arm and thanked me again. I asked her what the name of her baby was.

"Lilly," she said.

"Can I hold her?"

"Of course."

I made some funny noises and made Lilly smile, but when she realized she wasn't with her mom, she started to cry so I handed her back. Lilly's mom thanked me again and walked out to her car and drove away.

I sat down again to wait for my car. None of the other customers would even look at me. They were angry at me for making them look bad.

I realized then that for all the times the story of the Good Samaritan has been told, they always leave out the most important part. Which is, if you want to help someone, you can't care what your friends and neighbors are going to say about it afterwards. You know, like how foolish you were or how out of touch with reality you are, or if they complain that people are always taking advantage of you. You can't care about any of that.

The old man who'd recently come in sat down next to me. "Did you just help pay part of that young woman's bill?" he asked.

"Yes."

"Can I give you twenty dollars so I can be a part of this generous act of kindness."

"Yeah, I guess so."

He opened his checkbook and began to fill it in. "Who shall I make this out to?"

"Daniel Winchester."

He glanced up at me and studied my face. "By any chance are you related to the Winchester who used to be the janitor at the elementary school in Ashland?"

"Yes, he was my grandfather. Why do you ask?"

"I knew him! I was a teacher at the school. You look a lot like him. He was like you too. Always giving to others. You know what? He must be very proud of you."

"You think so?"

"I do. I'm sure of it. That's the way he was. He was always helping someone. I guess as custodian he knew what families in town were having a hard time. He helped hundreds of people. But most people in town never knew about it."

I smiled. Suddenly I felt better than I had for a long time.

"Thank you for telling me that." I shook his hand. We talked for the next half hour until they told him his car was done. And then he gave me his address and left.

Ten minutes later my car was done.

When I got in my car, I had a big smile on my face. Once again, for me, life was good.

Now I knew what the focus of my life was going to be.

Chapter Twelve

few days later DeAnna told Quentin that she wasn't going to marry him. When I asked why, she said, "I don't want to settle for second best. Besides, the truth is, I don't love him as much as I love you."

"So, that means you'd marry me, right?"

"Some day maybe, when the time is right."

The way I looked at it the only thing that was standing in the way of me marrying DeAnna was my legal problems. But in June, with the passage of a general amnesty bill for illegal aliens, all charges against me were dropped. And I was, once again, a free man.

The other good news in my life is that DeAnna was home for the summer.

"We could get married this summer," I said as the two of us weeded my mom's garden in the back yard.

"Yes, we could. Is that what you want?"

"Yeah, it is."

"You could go on a mission too."

"I'm serving a mission now," I said.

"I know you are. You could serve another mission."

"I don't want to go on a mission and come back and find you married to somebody else."

"I guess we would have to trust Father in Heaven that things would work out for the best for both of us whatever happened."

"I'm not sure I can do that," I said.

"I'm sure it wasn't convenient for the Good Samaritan to stop and give aid to a stranger."

"What does that have to do with going on a mission?"

"You figure it out."

"I hate it when people say that."

My mom was also weeding near us.

"I would very much like to go in your bedroom with you now, is that okay?" DeAnna asked.

"What?" I asked, panicking that my mom had heard what she'd just said.

"Just for a minute." She turned to my mom. "Is that okay?"

"Well, since DeAnna is the one asking, I'm sure it would be okay. I'll take these strawberries in and wash them while you two do that."

I'd previously told her what I'd done with the broom from the grade school where my grandfather worked as a custodian. But she'd never seen it on my wall.

"Why do you have this broom on your wall?" she asked as we looked at the broom setting horizontal in its own frame on my wall.

"You know the answer to that question."

"Answer it anyway."

"Because it reminds me of my grandfather."

"What do you want to remember about him?"

I cleared my throat. "That he wanted me to serve a mission."

"Okay. Anything else?"

I sighed. "That he spent his life serving others."

"That's who you are, Dan. That's what you'll continue to be. That's why I didn't marry Quentin. It's one of the things I love about you. So,

I think your decision about a mission is already made, isn't it?"

I walked over and touched the handle of the push broom, and then turned to look at DeAnna. "I guess maybe it is."

We walked back into the kitchen where my mom was dishing out some fresh strawberries for us.

DeAnna and I sat down at the table.

"Mom, I'm going on a mission," I told her.

She smiled and looked at DeAnna. "Well, that was fast. How did you do that?"

"She cheated," I joked.

Even though I'd made the decision to serve a mission, I still agonized over the possibility of losing DeAnna to some other guy while I was gone.

"Don't you trust me?" she asked.

"You I trust. I just don't trust all the guys you'll be dazzling while I'm gone."

"How about you go on your mission, and when I turn 21, I'll go on a mission."

"But then I'll have to wait for you to get back," I complained.

"So, start college."

That's what we did. In September, I left home to serve a Spanish speaking mission in the New York New York South mission. By the time I'd been out a year, she was called to serve a Spanish speaking mission in Ecuador, where her family had come from.

We stayed in contact all through our missions. The e-mails we traded were seldom pledges of love and devotion. They were about the work we did as missionaries. It added a new dimension to our relationship that we both treasured.

After my mission I began taking classes at BYU in Provo. To help pay for my education, I worked early mornings as a custodian on campus. I took pride in my work and wondered if my grandfather was pleased I was doing what he'd done his whole life.

My e-mails to DeAnna after I'd been released were mostly about my classes, but one I wrote about what I'd been thinking about, which was the parable of the Good Samaritan. This is what I wrote:

I do understand that the parable of the Good Samaritan is just a story. But even so, like so many parables, it can reveal other lessons. What I've been thinking about lately is that this business traveler didn't do just one act of service when he came across the man left to die by others. It must have been a part of his life. Which means he had helped others before that occasion. You can't say I'm going to help somebody some day. You have to say what can I do to help someone today? Lately I've included that in my prayers. I ask for opportunities to help others. And on the days I do that, I am surprised at the opportunities that come to me. The Savior doesn't want just one spectacular service act from us that we can tell in sacrament meeting talks throughout our lives. He wants service to others to be an integral part of our life. And that's what I'm trying to do now.

DeAnna wrote back: *Thank you for reminding me of the importance of looking for opportunities to serve every day. I will work on this every day.*

Oh, one more thing. I have seen this quality of service in you from the first day I met you. That is why I would be happy to be a part of your life. Because I know your focus is on service.

Finally DeAnna's mission ended.

Her parents invited me to go with them to pick her up at the airport.

It's still hard for me to describe my feelings at first seeing her. It wasn't what I'd imagined it would be. I thought it would be a return of the kind of feelings of love I'd had for her since high school. But that wasn't it. It was feelings of admiration for her as a missionary. That she'd been every bit as good as I'd been and most likely better. The sister missionaries in my mission had been amazing. I had often admired how effective they were in teaching the gospel. And so I realized she had been just like them.

I didn't want to throw romance into this greeting. She deserved to be respected and honored for the service she'd given. And my giving her a big hug or kissing her on the cheek would not have set the right tone.

After she'd hugged her parents, she turned to me. I shook her hand and said, "Welcome home, Sister Ortiz. We're so proud of the service you've given."

She smiled. "Thank you, Elder Winchester."

For the most part, I was just part of the family for the rest of the day. By that I mean I didn't ask to speak to her alone. I listened intently to everything she had to say. I guess anyone watching us might have thought I was either her brother or a cousin.

After dinner, she visited with our stake president and was released. But even that didn't change the way we interacted with each other.

She kept yawning after that so I told her I was going home. I asked if I could see her the next day.

"Could we have scripture study together in the morning?" she asked.

"Yeah, sure, that would be great."

"Sometimes on P-day, the missionaries would get together and play soccer," she said. "Would you like to do that?"

"I would. If this is a P-day, do we have to wash clothes and shop together too?"

She smiled. "Probably not."

"We could do the studying and the soccer at the park. What time shall I pick you up?"

"Seven thirty."

"You sure?"

"I'm sure. I don't want to waste the day sleeping."

I laughed. "I really hope that part of you changes."

When I pulled into her driveway the next morning at seven thirty, she was sitting on her steps reading the Book of Mormon in Spanish. She had a soccer ball next to her.

We ended up sitting at a picnic table. We read out loud a few chapters from Alma in the Book of Mormon.

And then we decided we needed a break. We stood up and made our way to a clearing. She placed the ball on the ground. "Are you as bad at soccer as you used to be?"

"No, I'm actually very good."

"I doubt it. Gringos can't play soccer. Come here, Gringo! Try and get the ball from me."

She ran down the field guiding the ball with her feet.

I caught up with her. She stopped running and taunted me. I made an awkward attempt to get the ball from her, but in the process kicked her in the shin.

"Ow! That hurt!"

The good news was that I now had control of the ball. "Hey, that's soccer. If you're going to cry, get off the field, you big baby."

Her eyes flashed, and she chased me. I was able to outmaneuver her, and we finally stopped to catch our breath. "Okay, you might be a little better than you used to be," she said.

"On my mission we practiced on P-day. And then, on Saturdays we played a game with our investigators and new converts."

"Really? I actually *worked* on my mission," she said with a smile.

"Yeah, yeah, I've heard that before."

We sat down to rest. But I kept the ball.

"How many baptisms did you have?" she asked.

"Nineteen."

"I had forty-seven," she said.

"And how many of those forty-seven did you personally actually baptize?" I asked.

She started laughing. "What a cheap shot."

"Hey, give me a break. I was desperate."

She looked at her watch. "For the next ten minutes we're only going to speak Spanish."

"Why?"

"*Por qué?*" she said to remind me to speak in Spanish.

At first she talked about things I would have known because of teaching the gospel to nonmembers. But after a few minutes, she began using words I'd never used the whole time I was on a mission.

At one point she ended a sentence with, "*persona que detiene el tráfico para permitir que los escolares crucen la calle.*" She started laughing. "What does that mean?"

I had no idea. "Well, that means—"

She stopped me. "Two words in English. That's it. That's all you get."

"What was that again?" I asked.

She said it again, but this time twice as fast. "Two words, Gringo. Two words." She looked at her watch. "Time's up. Sorry, you lose."

"What does it mean?"

"Crossing guard!" She started laughing.

"That is so not fair!"

"All's fair in love and war, my friend," she said.

"Which is this, love or war?"

"I'll tell you in a few days."

From the first time I saw her when we were in high school, I had loved just looking at her beautiful face. Her mission had enhanced her appearance, and now I couldn't take my eyes off her.

"So, what do we do now, Sister Ortiz?"

"You mean this afternoon?"

"No, I mean for the rest of our lives. *Quiero casarme contigo pronto,*" I said, hoping that meant that I wanted to marry her soon. It wasn't a part of the Spanish we used in teaching nonmembers.

"Are you serious?"

"Yeah, I am."

"Is this a proposal?"

"It could be."

"So where's the ring? Where's the flowers? How come you're not kneeling down in front of me?"

"I can do the whole bit, just not this afternoon." I paused. "Especially if I know you'll say yes."

"You want me to tell you what my answer will be before you ask the question?"

"Yeah, basically, that's it."

She thought about it. "No, I want you to worry."

"Okay, I will worry, until, how about tomorrow night?"

"Yes, worry until then."

And so I proposed Sunday night. First in English. And then, as a test, she made me propose to her in Spanish.

"Si, gracias," she said.

"So, can we kiss now?"

She scowled.

"What?" I complained.

"Give me a few days, okay? I need to get used to not being a missionary."

I am happy to report she made a quick adjustment. Only a matter of hours instead of days.

Two months later, in August, the Four Amigos were together again on our wedding day. At lunch in a restaurant between the temple ceremony and the reception, Chad, Jonathan, DeAnna, and I sang *The Ballad of the Three Amigos*. The effect was enhanced because Chad had borrowed four fancy black sombreros from the Theater Department's prop room at BYU.

We then invited Chad's wife Paige and Jonathan's wife Emma up and tried to sing for them *My Little Buttercup* from the movie. We never finished the song because we were all laughing so hard.

My biggest surprise at our reception was that Maria and her two kids, Gabriel and Kristina, and a two-year-old baby along with her husband, Eduardo, showed up. Chad had contacted Maria and invited them.

Their kids were so grown up, but they still loved the Four Amigos. And we loved them too. We gave each other big hugs. All of us spoke Spanish at first, mainly because we wanted to show off. But then we switched to English, and they showed us how well they'd learned the new language.

Maria told us they were living in Tucson and that they were working toward citizenship. Eduardo had a good job, too, and they were all very active in the Church.

Just before the reception ended, Maria and Eduardo asked to talk to me privately. Maria surprised me by repaying all the rest of the money I'd loaned her, along with the interest it would have earned if it had been left in the bank.

"You don't have to do this," I said.

"Yes, I do. You were my angel when I needed help."

Before they left, we all hugged them again. Kristina and Gabriel clung to me and said they loved me. I told them I loved them, too. After they left, I was trying to not let anyone, especially Chad, know how moved I'd been by their visit.

As I watched them drive away, DeAnna slipped her hand into mine. "This is why I loved you then, and why I love you now," she said.

"I'm the lucky one then, aren't I? I love you more than I can say."

Now, five years later, the Four Amigos are scattered all over the world. DeAnna and I are living in Brooklyn where I'm attending Columbia Law School. Chad and Paige live in California where Chad works in product development for Disney Studios. Johnny B and his wife Emma are in Chicago where he's in med school.

Each of us have our career goals, but underlying that, for all of us, is a strong desire to serve others. Mainly because when we were seniors in high school, we learned how serving others can enrich your life.

Right now, as friends, we have to content ourselves with e-mails, text messages, and phone calls. But Chad is planning a reunion for us next summer, along with our combined total of four kids, one from DeAnna and me, two from Chad and Paige, and one on the way from Johnny B and Emma.

Chad keeps us informed of the things he's planned for our reunion. I think I speak for all of us when I say how little we're looking forward to the human wheelbarrow race and the water balloon toss. But what can you say? That's Chad for you.

We are still, and hope to always be, the Four Amigos. Or, if you count Paige and Emma, the Six Amigos. And if you count our kids, who knows how many Amigos there will eventually be? That's the way it should be.

I have a plan now that when each of our kids graduates from Primary, I will give him or her a small piece of my grandfather's push broom, just to remind them that we're put on this earth to serve others.

Just like the Good Samaritan.

About the Author:

Jack Weyland is one of the best-known authors of young adult fiction for Latter-day Saint audiences, having written over twenty best selling novels. His first novel *Charly* was made into a movie in 2002. For further information, go to www.jackweyland.com.